HEALING MONTANA LOVE

BEAR GRASS SPRINGS, BOOK ELEVEN

RAMONA FLIGHTNER

GRIZZLY DAMSEL PUBLISHING

CHAPTER 1

Mountain Bluebird Ranch, Montana Territory; May 1889

Charlotte Ingram stood on the bunkhouse stoop at the Mountain Bluebird Ranch near the town of Bear Grass Springs, Montana. A meadowlark warbled, and she gave thanks the breeze blew in the opposite direction today, sending the barn's stench away from the bunkhouse. Although she understood she should be thankful for the pungent odors—as it meant there was milk and butter and food to eat—she had yet to become accustomed to ranch life.

Although she had been on the ranch since February, the months seemed to crawl by. First because she was in a miasma of pain and despair. Now because every day consisted of a monotony of similar chores. She took a deep breath of the fresh air, closing her eyes with delight, as she scented the faint hint of lilacs on the breeze. Finally Montana's version of spring was arriving. Wisps of reddish-blond hair tickled her cheeks, as they fluttered in the faint breeze, having escaped the braid down her back. Her sensible faded blue calico dress flapped at her ankles, and she tugged her serviceable shawl around her shoulders.

With a sigh, she returned to the kitchen to prepare another meal for the men. Although they were courteous, few were overtly flirtatious, and none crossed the line into impropriety. The men knew they would be fired and forced to find work on another less prosperous ranch if they harassed her. Saying a silent prayer of thanksgiving for men like Frederick Tompkins and his foreman, Slims, for ensuring she was respected, she hummed while she worked.

Soon Charlotte was lost to her work, focusing on preparing a large apple crumble from the last of the previous year's crop, while bread baked in the oven, and stew bubbled on the stove. As someone tapped her arm, she shrieked, spinning and jabbing with the knife in her hand. "Stay away," she gasped.

The ranch hand Dalton held up his hands, his blue eyes rounded with surprise, as he barely backed away in time to prevent a stabbing. The sound of his shirt tearing filled the otherwise silent room. "Miss Ingram," he murmured in a low voice. "I didn't mean to startle you. You were woolgathering." He shrugged, as he took another step backward, his alert gaze noting how her arm quivered. "Why don't you put down the knife? No one will harm you here." He stood half a foot taller than her, and his long arms could have easily manhandled the knife from her. However, he did not attempt to touch her again.

In an instant, Charlotte flushed beet red and spun to turn away from him. The muffled sound of her stifling a sob carried, and he took a hesitant step in her direction. However, he couldn't see the knife, and he had no desire for her aim to prove more accurate this time. "Miss Ingram?"

"Forgive me," she gasped, her sherry-colored eyes filled with humiliation, as she looked at him over her shoulder. "I was foolish. If you leave me your shirt, I'll mend it." She bowed her head, as she fought to control her quivering. The knife clattered to the countertop beside the stove.

He took a few ponderous steps, pulling out a chair with a loud scrape, as though to indicate he were a fair distance from her. "I wondered if any coffee was left in the pot."

A hysterical laugh burst forth, and she slammed her hand over her mouth to prevent any further inappropriate sounds from emerging. However, she knew she was on the verge of giving in to her fears of never feeling secure, and she could not prevent the hot scald of tears as they poured down her cheeks.

"Miss?" he murmured, suddenly standing behind her again. At the soft touch to her shoulder, she flinched and then relaxed. "Miss, you're safe here. You know the men are loyal to you."

She refused to turn and face him. In a stuttering voice, she rasped, "No, they're loyal to the Missus. The two Missuses. They tolerate me. And give me a wide berth because they don't want to lose their jobs." She took a long breath, finally corralling her out-of-control emotions. Reaching out a shaking hand, she grasped a coffee cup and filled it. "I believe you like it black." She turned to hand it to him, refusing to meet his gaze.

"Look at me," he whispered. When she kept her eyes downcast, he murmured, "Please."

At the entreaty, her gaze flew to his, and she frowned in confusion. Men gave her orders. They didn't make polite requests which she could refuse. She met his worried gaze—his blue eyes with wrinkles at the corners—as he focused all his attention on her. His brown hair was scrunched down, like he'd just taken off his hat, and she fought an irrational urge to run her hands through it.

"I know someone hurt you, Miss Ingram. It's plain to see.

But not all men are scoundrels." He paused as he reached to accept the cup of coffee from her. "One day you'll come to realize you can trust more than yourself." With a nod of his head, he left.

Charlotte stood in frozen wonder for a long moment, wondering if she had imagined the entire interlude. *Interlude?* She berated herself for being fanciful. Her imagination was what had led to her nearly assaulting the man. With a shiver, she faced the stove again, determined to forget Dalton. To forget his solicitude. His kindness. His constancy. For she knew it was always a pretense to entice a woman to do something she might have had the sense to decline.

She took a deep breath to calm her nerves. Instead his alluring scent teased her senses. Musky, with a hint of sandalwood cologne, mixed with sweat and the scent of horses. With a huff, she turned to the window and took a gulp of the clean spring air, determined to ignore any and all attraction for a ranch hand named Dalton.

Dalton stood in the yard, sipping his cup of coffee, his mind filled with images of Charlotte. Voluptuous, graceful, beautiful Charlotte. Her fine silky-looking red-gold hair never managed to stay tamed by a braid or a bun, and wisps of it always framed her rounded cheeks. He fought a constant yearning to run a work-roughened hand over her enticing hair but knew it would be wholly inappropriate.

Although he had spent a few moments with her when she first arrived at the ranch last year, he had suspected she was angling after his good friend and boss, Slims. When that proved to be a false assumption, after she ran off in December, he had forced himself to forget any fanciful imaginings he'd had about her. Then, when she returned a few months later, bruised in spirit and skittish of her own shadow, he had told himself that he merely wanted to protect her from suffering any more harm.

"Fool," he muttered to himself. When he saw his friend and foreman approaching, Dalton grunted a greeting. Slims was the largest man he'd ever met at six and a half feet tall and barrel chested. Although he could run the ranch through sheer domination, he was a gentle giant. Unless someone threatened people Slims cared for, then he was fierce.

"Who's a fool?" Slims asked.

Grinning as he took a sip of coffee, Dalton shrugged. "I am."

"I could have told you that," Slims said with a wry chuckle. His alert gaze roved over the outbuildings and the fields closest to the big house. "There's plenty of fresh grass this year. The cattle will eat well."

Dalton shrugged and slurped another sip. He'd never found it necessary to expound on the obvious. He slanted a covert glance at his friend, watching as Slims's entire demeanor softened at the sight of Davina, Slims's wife, walking toward them. "Missus," Dalton said with a deferential nod.

"Hello, Dalton," she said with a smile that faded into one of confusion. "What happened to yer shirt?" She reached out to finger the hole on the left side of his belly. "Did someone try to stab ye?" Although a tiny woman at barely five feet tall, she and her giant of a husband did not make an incongruous pair. Somehow they were a perfect match. Seeing them together filled Dalton with an intense yearning.

"I startled Charlotte, Miss Ingram." He shrugged once more, as though a near stabbing were a normal everyday occurrence. "It was entirely my fault."

Davina squinted her brown eyes, as she flicked a quick glance at her husband. "When someone takes me by surprise,

I jump. Or yelp. I dinna come at them with a knife." Her Scottish accent was as strong as the day she had arrived at the ranch in January, four months ago. Although she and Slims had had a whirlwind romance, they had found a deep and abiding love.

Slims rocked back on his heels. "Come on, Dav. You know there's much we don't understand about her."

Dalton felt his hackles rise at the implied criticism of Charlotte, although he knew it was justified. Charlotte had attempted to harm their marriage in February. "I thought you were no longer bitter," he murmured.

"And I thought you were more sensible," Slims shot back.

"Boys," Davina said with a wry smile. "There's nae need to argue. I can mend Dalton's shirt afore anyone asks more questions, and we now ken to make a wee bit of noise if Charlotte's back is turned to us. One of ye should inform Frederick, so he and Sorcha are aware."

"I will," Dalton said, as he took the final sip of his cup of coffee. "If you'll wait a moment, Missus." He nodded to her, leaving her to flirt with her husband on this fine morning, as he slipped inside to change into his other shirt. When he returned, he handed the torn shirt to her and motioned for her to walk beside him, as they approached the big house.

The ranch was a combination of three homesteads the Tompkinses had cobbled together in the mid-1860s, along with other parcels of land they had purchased over the years. Frederick Tompkins's grandparents, Harold and Irene, had moved here from Fort Benton with their son, his wife, and children to stake their claims, prove them up, and turn their dreams into reality. Now they had a thriving cattle ranch, and Dalton had found the family he'd yearned for, since he'd lost his in the Civil War.

Rather than follow Davina inside to chat with her as she mended his shirt, he saw Frederick looking over the fields.

He nodded at Davina and ambled in that direction. Frederick was the youngest of the Tompkins brothers at thirty-four, and he had a deep love of the land, which his two older brothers had never discovered. A tall lanky broad-shouldered man, Frederick had attracted the attention of all the eligible single women in Bear Grass Springs. However, the only woman who made his blue eyes shine bright was his wife, Sorcha. Now he stood at the fence, his hat tipped forward to shield his eyes.

"Beautiful morning, Dalton," Frederick said, as Dalton sidled up beside him. "How are the new hands workin' out?"

Dalton chuckled. "Fine. Dixon's runnin' them through their paces." He paused as he saw Frederick smile at the thought of the young hand showing anyone the ropes. "He seems to enjoy it."

"He would," Frederick said, his eyes crinkling with merriment. "He's probably sick of you, Slims, and Shorty ridin' herd on him all the time. Must be nice for him to have the chance to turn the focus onto someone else."

Dalton tilted his head, momentarily considering the other two ranch hands, Shorty and Dixon, who worked at the ranch year-round with him and Slims. Shorty was Slims's best friend and barely taller than Davina. Shorty was an expert horseman and cattleman, and had seen the ranch through difficult times. Dixon was as eager as an untrainable puppy and had the energy to go with. Dalton had always thought the four of them combined made a good team.

"I thought you'd be on the range today," Frederick said, a slight note of censure in his voice. Although a fair and caring employer, he expected his men to work hard.

"I had thought to, but Miss Ingram was out of sorts." When Frederick stared at him inquisitively, Dalton murmured, "One of the men mentioned Mrs. MacKinnon's newspaper article about the Copper Kings in Butte.' He

7

paused, as though recalling breakfast and how pale Charlotte had become. "I thought she'd faint dead away." He shrugged. "It didn't seem right leaving her this mornin', Boss, not after you told us you thought we needed to protect her once she arrived here."

"A Copper King?" Frederick muttered. "Is that why he was worried?"

When Frederick stared at him a long moment, as though deciding if Dalton would answer his question, Dalton bit back a swear. "Who?"

Frederick sighed and rubbed at his forehead. "That damn lawyer. He uses his thousand-dollar words and charming smile to convince you to do something, but you don't even know why you're doing it." He pounded a hand on the fence, making the wood rattle. "He never explained why he wanted Charlotte to hide away here on the ranch with us. Now I wonder if he was worried about a Copper King coming after her."

Perplexed at the rancor in Frederick's voice, Dalton said, "I thought you liked Mr. Clark."

Warren Clark was Bear Grass Springs's resident lawyer and married to one of the town's healers, Helen. Warren was also a close friend of the MacKinnons. As Sorcha was a MacKinnon, it meant he was automatically a friend of Frederick's. However, Frederick had also befriended Helen, offering her a place of refuge, when she and Warren were having a difficult time earlier in their relationship.

"I like the man fine but sometimes lose patience with the lawyer part of him," Frederick said with a wry quirk of his lips. "What else is there? You wouldn't seek me out because you didn't ride out today."

"Miss Ingram is easily startled, Boss. When I went into the kitchen for a cup of coffee, she didn't hear me and would have stabbed me if I hadn't backed away."

Frederick's gaze roved over Dalton, nodding in reassurance to find his man unharmed. "You unarmed her?"

"No, I backed away in time. I thought you should warn Sorcha. I wouldn't want anything to happen to her or the twins."

Frederick's gaze hardened at the thought. "Perhaps Miss Ingram should leave the ranch. I won't risk my family's safety, Dalton."

Dalton nodded. He rested his arms on the top rail and leaned against it, as he looked out at the vast landscape. Nearby green grass and rolling fields filled the vista, whereas dramatic mountain peaks rose up to frame the valley in the distance. Snow hugged the peaks, although each day more and more of it melted away. A creek surrounded with willows and cottonwood trees meandered through the verdant valley. "I understand, Boss. But she doesn't strike me as a woman out to cause harm. Not now. She's still desperate. And in need of someone to help her. You're offering her refuge, and I keep thinkin' she's in need of it."

Frederick sighed and took his hat off to slap it on his thigh before jamming it on his head again. "Perhaps," he groused, "but how long did Warren expect me to continue to offer her a safe haven? I thought she'd be here a few weeks. Maybe a month. It's close to four months since she arrived." He paused and cast an assessing look at his ranch hand. "You're quick to come to her defense."

Dalton nodded. "I'd like to think, if my sisters had lived, someone would have looked after them too." His jaw tightened, and his gaze hardened. "And whoever did this to Miss Ingram should pay, Boss."

Sighing again, Frederick nodded. "Aye," he murmured, repeating a word his Scottish wife often said and that they had all picked up, "they should. No woman should be afraid of her own shadow." He slapped Dalton on his back. "Do what you feel's right. I trust you." He ambled away in the direction of his horse barn.

Dalton watched him for a moment before sighing, as he considered Charlotte's reaction this morning. With a shake of his head, he feared this was just the prelude to the storm.

That evening Dalton sat on the front porch of the bunkhouse in one of the rocking chairs, listening to an owl hoot and to coyotes yip in the distance. He hoped none had a notion to dine on one of their calves, but he knew it was the nature of things to lose a few head each year to them. With a sigh, he closed his eyes and listened as Charlotte first hummed and then sang to herself, while cleaning up the kitchen.

Although the men had offered to help her clean after the meals, she had been astute enough to realize that a few of them would hope for some form of compensation. A walk. A larger portion of stew. Perhaps even a kiss. Rather than fending off any disappointments, she had declined all help and had worked hard to feed the men three meals a day. Dalton had appreciated her discretion, although he worried that one of the newer men would continue to press her for more than she wished to offer. Life on the ranch was lonely, and one rarely found a single handsome woman.

The bunkhouse was a long building with a small covered front porch. Inside, a long hallway connected the kitchen at the far end to the right to the large gathering room to the left, with three private bedrooms in between. Past the gathering room was a large bunkroom where the seasonal workers slept. As the cook, Miss Ingram's room was directly beside the kitchen. Shorty and Dixon shared the room beside hers, and Dalton's was next to the gathering room.

Dalton used to share his room with Slims, but, when he married Davina, Slims moved out to a nearby cabin. Now one such cabin remained empty, in case another of the year-round hands married.

Although Dalton trusted Shorty, Dixon, and Slims implicitly, he didn't know the men well who worked on the ranch each season. Thus he had angled his chair on the porch near the window, so he could hear the goings-on in the kitchen. If he heard Miss Ingram sing, well, that was simply an added bonus.

Charlotte never joined him outside, and he knew she had retreated to her room when the kitchen fell silent. She never mingled with any of the ranch hands, and Dalton had ensured that she had a sturdy latch on her door when she moved in. To date, none of the interim ranch hands had made any inappropriate advances toward her, and Dalton hoped their respect for her never wavered.

Closing his eyes, he fought memories of other evenings, when he sat in quiet companionship, listening to a woman sing as she puttered around him. After three years, her face was becoming blurry, but the sense of home, of the peace she had always engendered when he thought of her, readily filled him. The pervasive longing he had felt when he saw Davina and Slims together overcame him again. "Mary," he breathed, his breath catching, as he longed to forget those last moments as he watched her and their baby die. Although the agony wasn't as acute today, the ache for all he had lost was ever present.

He rested his head against the back of his rocking chair, silently berating himself. Dalton knew he should be used to being alone. After his family had been brutally taken from him during the Civil War, he had struck out West. After years where he had thought he would wander forever, he had been fortunate enough to drift onto the Mountain Bluebird

Ranch. Harold and Irene still ran it at the time, and they took him on for seasonal help.

He smiled with his eyes closed, as he remembered that first summer. Although he had thought he knew all there was to know about working a farm, he soon realized he knew next to nothing about cattle ranching and precious little about breeding horses. To this day, he didn't know what induced the Tompkinses to take him on as a full-time hand, but he would never forget their generosity.

Although he often lost patience with Dixon, the youngest permanent ranch hand, Dalton saw so much of his youthful self in Dix. The eagerness to please. The belief that there was no promise of tomorrow, so he had better enjoy today. The desire to learn everything he could with the hope of becoming indispensable. Even though he had tempted fate and had believed for a short time in the promise of tomorrows, Dalton knew Dix was right. There was no reason to worry about tomorrow, for today was all he had been guaranteed.

Charlotte glanced out the window, surreptitiously noting that Dalton continued to rock and doze on the porch, as she worked and sang in the kitchen. She had first seen him outside one evening as the weather warmed, and she suspected that he always sat nearby, as though to fend off any undesired attention. Flushing with appreciation for his chivalry, she continued to putter around the kitchen. After today's near stabbing, she had feared he would wash his hands of her and would forego any further attempt to safeguard her.

Since her arrival on the ranch in February, he had been her unofficial guardian, shadowing her, as she slowly decided she did not want to die. That it was worth fighting to live, even though the life she thought she'd have, had dreamed of having, would never be her reality. She turned away from the window, as though banishing that thought and began to sing again.

She had discovered that singing soothed a sorrow deep in her soul. With a mournful smile, she also knew it brought joy to her audience of one. For some reason, that small knowledge filled her with a sense of accomplishment and delight.

When she finished her song, she looked around the tidy kitchen and nodded with satisfaction. Although working as a cook had never been her dream as a girl, she knew any type of work was to be valued. Too often women had far-too-few options.

Picking up her lantern, she whispered a silent, "Sweet dreams," to Dalton and moved on soundless feet to her room, where she prayed her nightmares gave her one night's respite.

CHAPTER 2

Charlotte tended to tune out the men's chatter at every meal, and she did so again, as she set out the evening meal for them to eat. They sat at a long table with benches on either side. No one sat at the head of the table, unless Slims joined them for dinner. As foreman, he liked to join them once or twice a week, if possible, to chat with the men and to socialize with them away from work. As he no longer lived in the bunkhouse, due to his marriage to Davina in February, it was one of the few ways he had to spend time with them when the men weren't working.

Charlotte thought it curious the foreman would be so concerned about keeping a close bond with his men. However, she rarely attempted to make conversation with the man, as he still hadn't fully forgiven her for the havoc she had wreaked upon her return in February. Thankfully his wife was more understanding, although Charlotte supposed it was helpful Davina was Sorcha's cousin. Everything was easier when you were related to the owner.

Battling bitterness at her persistent lot in life, Charlotte set out baskets of cornbread before she ladled up bowls of chili. Reluctantly she listened in, as the men chattered around her.

"Shorty, are we goin' to the Founders' Dance in a few weeks?" one of the new hands asked.

"Dix, do you think pretty girls are gonna be there to dance with, or is it a waste of money to go to the barber?" asked another newcomer to the ranch, an eagerness in his expression.

"It's always a waste for you," Shorty said with a teasing glint in his eyes, as he winked at Dalton.

"Dalt, did you hear about that fancy lady come to stay at the hotel? Heard tell she's married to one of the Copper Kings!" another said, as he fidgeted, eyeing the cornbread.

Charlotte froze as the conversation continued around her. The ladle was in one hand, half raised, with the bowl tilted precariously to the side, as her breath emerged in pants. A buzzing began in her ears, and she felt on the verge of fainting. Suddenly her world went black, and a blissful numbness overtook her.

"Miss Ingram!" Dalton bellowed, as he launched himself toward her, when she swayed and fell backward. He caught her just as she was about to crash to the floor, cradling her head against his leg which he thrust out to break her fall. Grunting with pain as she landed hard, he held her while sitting on the floor.

After assuring that she was as well as she could be, he looked to Shorty and Dixon. "Get Slims and Boss. Now." They raced away. Glaring at the other men, Dalton said, "Take a piece of bread, a bowl of chili, and eat somewhere else. I don't care where. But you will stop staring at her."

The men muttered their agreement, hastily snatching up

food and leaving the kitchen. Soon Dalton was alone with an insensate Charlotte in his arms. "Come on, Miss Ingram. Wake up. Nothin's so bad that you need to pull such shenanigans." He closed his eyes, as he attempted to still his racing heart, kissing her on her head, while his hands rubbed her back to convey some comfort. Anything so that she would know she was safe. "Come on, love," he whispered. "Wake up."

"Shenanigans?" she murmured in a disgruntled voice, as she struggled against his hold. "Do you believe me so vain that I would act like this for no reason?"

He smiled as she opened her beautiful sherry-colored eyes. "No, but I didn't know what else to say. It's not every day I catch a woman on the verge of a faint." He sobered as he saw terror fill her gaze. "You're safe here, Miss Ingram. You know Boss and the men will protect you."

Closing her eyes, she snuggled into his embrace for a moment before stiffening, suddenly realizing what she was doing. She pushed at him, attempting to force herself up to stand.

"Take it easy. You've had a fright for some reason. Don't overdo it."

"What must you think of me?" she asked, as she held up a hand to shield her face from him. "You must consider me the most immoral woman you've ever met."

He chuckled and shook his head. "You've never been to the Boudoir, Miss." At her deep flush, he bit back what more he would have said. "Forgive me. I shouldn't tease you." At the sound of running men, he looked to the door. "Boss," he said. "Slims. Sorry to interrupt dinner at the big house." He looked around their shoulders to see Davina had raced along behind them.

"She really did faint," Davina said with a small frown of surprise.

Charlotte struggled in earnest to rise and to be released from Dalton's hold. When Frederick and Slims took hold of an elbow each and hauled her up, she gasped and swayed on her feet. "Oh, give me a moment," she breathed. "I've never been so unsteady."

Dalton leaped up, and he held a hand to the small of her back. Leaning over her, he peered at her with avid concern. "Are you going to have another spell?"

She shook her head. "No. I don't know what came over me."

Davina stood there, and she shook her head, glowering with disapproval. "I dinna believe ye. I think ye do remember but want to continue to hide it from us all. Why no' be honest with us? With Frederick? He's protectin' ye an' doesna even ken why."

Charlotte looked around the kitchen and shook her head. "Not here. Please."

Frederick nodded. "Come. Let's go to the big house."

Dalton watched as Charlotte ran a hand over her dress and walked demurely past the men loitering on the front porch. With the open windows, Dalton understood her desire for privacy. Too many would have been privy to her private affairs. He walked behind her, wishing he had the right to escort her. To be the man she leaned on when she stumbled. Instead she reached for Frederick.

Upon entering the big house, Frederick motioned for her to sit on one of the settees, as he went in search of Sorcha. Everyone knew better than to call out for her, as none wanted to be responsible for waking the twins, if they had already gone down for the night.

Dalton angled himself so he could watch Charlotte's reaction to everything that was said but hoped his close perusal of her wasn't obvious. She sat, her hands clasped together on her lap, her head bowed, and he again wished he could sit beside her, whisper sweet words in her ear. Anything to ease her tension. Instead he acted as witness, waiting for the arrival of Sorcha.

Sorcha bustled into the room with food stains on her dress and her reddish-brown hair falling out of its pins. Her light-blue eyes held a fair amount of suspicion as she stared at Charlotte. Settling across from her on a matching settee, she smiled at Davina, who sat beside her. "So, Charlotte, it seems ye had a wee spell while cookin' dinner."

Charlotte nodded, her gaze remaining downcast. She took a deep breath, before raising her gaze to meet Sorcha's. "Your sister-in-law is a reporter. A good one, I'm told."

"Aye," Sorcha said, her brows furrowed in confusion, as though attempting to understand where Charlotte's story was going. Sorcha thought it common knowledge that she was the youngest MacKinnon sibling and that her youngest brother, Ewan, had married Jessamine, the town's reporter.

"She'd be able to discover a newcomer's identity in town. Her true identity. Not the one she wanted folks to believe." At Sorcha's nod, Charlotte heaved out a breath. "I have little money, but do you think she'd investigate something for me?"

With a wry smile, Sorcha said, "If 'twas an interestin' story, I ken Jessie'd pay ye for it." Her smile faded, as Charlotte paled at her attempt at teasing. "Will ye no' share with us what troubles ye? Ye've let it fester too long already."

Dalton stood stock-still, hoping Charlotte would speak. Praying she'd forget he and the other men were present, so Dalton could finally hear the truth. When she began to whisper in a halting voice, a surge of triumph raced through him. Now he would know the enemy. No longer would the foe be faceless and nameless. Now, finally, Dalton would be able to protect her.

"I was a fool. But you all know that. You all know my

greatest shame," she whispered in a halting voice. "You know I came here, claiming to be pregnant. Claiming it was Slims's." She bit her lip. "I'm sorry." Her voice quivered with remorse, as her gaze darted in his direction. "I would never have agreed with Wa ... with the plan, if I'd known of your interest in another."

"Warren's plan," Slims said with a nod. "I've known since February he had a hand in your precipitous arrival here."

Charlotte wrung her fingers together, the words leaving her in fits and starts. "I never should have left here in December. I'd thought I'd met the man of my dreams during trips to town. He was sweet and attentive. He wrote letters. I thought he loved me."

Dalton clamped his jaw shut from saying anything that would interrupt her story. However, he yearned to offer her comfort as she sat alone, in a roomful of people who were not her friends or family, baring her soul.

"I met him in late September," she whispered, "when we came back from the far homestead."

"Good riddance," Slims muttered emphatically, referencing the miserable summer they had spent sparring on the ranch. He and Charlotte had never seen eye to eye and had fought constantly, as she cooked for him and Shorty during the months they had spent there.

She flushed. "He was the opposite of you, and I thought that meant he loved me. Solicitous. Kind. Charming." She flushed red. "I didn't realize it was all a ploy to entice me to behave improperly. I believed his words. I ... acted in a way I shouldn't have. At the Harvest Dance. And I discovered, in December, that I was to have his child."

"'Tis why ye fled in December," Sorcha said.

"I knew he was in Butte then." Her gaze flit to Dalton, who had frozen at the mention of the mining city. "I knew I needed to find him. To share our good fortune. To raise our child together."

Dalton studied her, as she sat in dejected silence. "He was already married," he said in a cold, hard voice.

"Yes," she whispered. "Unfortunately his wife is a vindictive, jealous woman. And barren." She cleared her throat. "When I refused to agree to give her my baby, she invited me for tea." Charlotte flushed. "I've always been poor. My time here was one of the few periods of my life when I didn't have to worry about where I'd find my next meal. When I was with her, I ate too much. Drank too much tea."

"Why should that matter?" Frederick asked, a confused glance in Sorcha's direction.

"She hurt yer bairn, did she no'?" Sorcha asked in a soft voice, as she shared a long look with Davina. "She gave ye tea that would hurt yer bairn?" Sorcha glared at the men in the room as they swore their anger.

"That's what I was told." Silent tears coursed down her cheek, as she held her hands over her lower belly. "I was informed that, if anyone from his family ever found me again, they'd find a way to kill me. And that no one in this Territory or the entire West Coast would care about a poor woman's death. For he, ... my baby's father, ... was a man who would soon be a Copper King. And royalty can do what they like."

"She killed yer bairn and thinks to make ye feel guilty for it?" Davina hissed. "The witch." One of her hands instinctively rose to clasp Slims's, the other to cover her lower belly.

"Ain't no royalty here," Dixon sputtered out.

"Aye, but the rich have a funny way of forgettin' that," Shorty muttered, as he looked at Charlotte with sympathy.

Dalton stood silent, thinking through the conversation bandied about before supper that evening. About a fancy woman from Butte arriving in town. "You fear she's come to Bear Grass Springs. That she's looking for you again."

"Yes," Charlotte said. "And this time, she'll kill me."

Dalton stiffened at her proclamation. "Over my dead body," he rasped. He flushed when everyone turned to stare at him but did not take back his words. He nodded to Charlotte. "Miss Charlotte, you're safe here. Even if that woman is in town, she has no reason to come here, and she'll not be able to harm you here on the ranch."

Charlotte curved her shoulders into herself, as though protecting herself. "I have no right to expect you to do more than you've done."

Davina rose with a disgruntled murmur, moving to sit beside Charlotte. She wrapped an arm around Charlotte's shoulder, easing her close to her side in a comforting gesture. "*Shh*, dinna talk such nonsense. Ye ken we'll care for ye. We've been upset—Slims an' I—because ye refused to tell us the truth. Now that I ken how ye suffered and all ye fear, I would never hold that against ye."

"Nor would I," Slims said.

"We protect our own, Charlotte," Frederick said, while everyone else in the room murmured their agreement with his proclamation. When she gaped at him, he nodded. "Aye, you're one of us, now that you've trusted us with what happened." His jaw clenched. "If I'd known what occurred, what that libertine had done …" He clamped his jaw shut. "You wouldn't have been alone in December, Charlotte."

She stiffened her shoulders and spoke in a voice filled with forced bravado, as though unwilling to accept their compassion. "I had every right to leave. And I thought he wanted me."

Sorcha stared at her long and hard. "Ye believed we'd turn our backs on ye because ye were unwed and pregnant. Ye were desperate, and ye ran."

Charlotte raised and lowered her hands, as though to signal her despair and frustration, her bravado seeping away. She looked around the room, meeting the gaze of everyone present, as though searching for the one who would prove false their solidarity of understanding and compassion. Instead, all showed an earnestness and a regret at what she had suffered. Her gaze held Dalton's the longest, and she let out a quivering breath at the searing remorse in his expression. "Everyone knows it's always the woman's fault," she whispered.

"Bull," Dalton said. "You were an innocent seduced by an expert. He knew what he was doin'. An' he knew he wasn't free." His jaw ticked as he clamped it shut.

"You say he's a Copper King, Miss Ingram?" Slims asked, as he scratched his head. "I thought they were married. And a bit old for you."

Dalton watched as a soft flush covered her neck and cheeks. "No one judges you here, Miss."

She looked directly at him, as though overwhelmed by the number of people discovering the truth. As though she needed to focus solely on him to continue to talk about the betrayal she had suffered. "I know it makes me a naive fool. I should never have been taken in." She sniffled, as tears coursed down her cheeks. "I learned, when I arrived in Butte, that he's hoping to become rich, like Daly or Clark. He has minor claims and some wealth. But nothing to truly rival one of the Kings."

Davina held her hand. "But even that amount of riches was more than ye'd ever seen before, aye? Ever dreamed about?" She spoke in a soft voice, her gaze filled with compassionate understanding.

"Yes," Charlotte whispered. "I was blinded by riches."

"*Ach*, 'tis hard no' to be when ye've been poor," Sorcha said. "Especially if ye've no family to ground ye." She sighed and glared at Slims. "If ye'd no' fought so much with Slims, ye might have seen that we could have become yer family."

Charlotte choked on a sob, causing Dalton to fist his hands, as he fought every instinct to pull her into his arms and to soothe her. "We still can," Dalton said, causing everyone present to again gape at him. "Miss Ingram is here now. She's under Boss's protection."

Frederick stared at him assessingly. "It appears I haven't been paying attention."

Sorcha made a sound in the back of her throat, muttering, "Ye have, but ye were none pleased when ye did no' ken the truth." She rose and held out her hand to Frederick. "Come. We must check on the bairns." A subtle shake of her head quieted any protest Frederick might have attempted.

Davina stroked a hand down Charlotte's arm. "Dinna fash, Charlotte. All will turn out well. I ken everything seems bleak at the moment, but 'twill improve. I promise ye." She rose, linking her arm through Slims's, as they too departed for their nearby cabin.

Dalton met Shorty's gaze, as Shorty nodded at his friend and coworker, a silent vote for Dalton to remain here with Charlotte, until she was ready to return to the bunkhouse. Shorty and Dixon headed to the bunkhouse to eat dinner.

A fire crackled in the hearth, the only sound breaking the quiet in the large room after the exodus. Dalton remained standing, as though a sentry, near the edge of her settee. Finally he took a deep breath, before he asked in a soft voice, "Why didn't you tell me?" He fisted his hands at his sides as he stared at her, battling his instinctual need to sit beside her, to pull her close, and to comfort her. Instead he stood woodenly, his gaze inscrutable, as he waited for her to look at him.

"What was I to say?" she whispered with ducked head, the red in her hair glowing in the fire's light. "I was a fool."

"Ah, Lottie," he whispered, the use of his nickname for her causing her head to jerk up. He smiled gently as he moved closer to her. His hand rose to softly trace a line down her cheek, evoking a shiver. "We've all been fools for love. Some of us pay a higher price than others."

She sniffled, scooting away, her gaze defiant, as she wrapped her arms around her belly and hunched her shoulders. "I never want to feel that way again."

"In love?" he asked with a frown. "Or like a fool?" He took a half step in her direction, stilling before she felt as though he were crowding her. Backing up, he resumed his position in the corner. "I beg your pardon. I realize you have no desire for friendship with one such as me."

"One such as you?" she asked, staring at him in confusion. "I fear you have it backward." She pasted on an impersonal smile as she stared at him, as though he were nothing more than a ranch hand.

"Don't look at me like that." His eyes glowed with anger and despair. At her confused stare, he whispered, "As though I were nothing more than a man you make coffee for or set a plate in front of." He closed his eyes and took a step away from her to return to the bunkhouse. "Forgive me."

She rose, setting her small hand on his arm, the warmth of her fingers like a brand. "No," she entreated. "Don't leave me. When I know you are close, I feel safe." She ducked her head and whispered, "Safer."

He took a deep breath. "I would ask one thing of you." He waited, frowning as he saw the disappointment in her gaze. With a gentle smile, he murmured, "Don't feel shame for having dreamed."

Her eyes widened in shock at his words, a soft smile blooming.

At the sight of her smile, Dalton felt a tightness in his chest and knew he would cherish the memory of this moment forever. He traced a finger down her cheek again, motioning for her to walk in front of him, so he could escort her to the bunkhouse.

CHAPTER 3

That evening Dalton sat on the bunkhouse stoop, rocking as he stared at the moon. The other men were inside, playing cards, reading from five-and-dime novels, or attempting to scratch out letters to distant family members. Miss Sorcha encouraged all of them to write to family and had insisted the ranch would pay for the postage of all ranch hand letters, up to two letters a month per ranch hand. He wondered if they knew how fortunate they were to have someone to write to.

Dalton closed his eyes a moment, as he rested his head against the back of the rocking chair, listening to the men chatter away, worse than magpies. Although he knew women had the reputation of being the worst gossips, he had long suspected the men who he worked with were far worse than any women he knew. The main difference being that men rarely had any desire to hurt another with their prattle. None of the hands seemed overly concerned about Charlotte fainting in the kitchen, as she had appeared to quickly recover from her swoon, although a few had cast curious glances in his direction.

When the bunkhouse door creaked, he slitted open an eye to see who interrupted his quiet interlude. At the sight of Charlotte creeping out with her beautiful hair tied in a loose braid that nearly reached her bottom, he sat upright. "Miss Ingram."

She jumped, swallowing a shriek. "Oh, you startled me, Mr. Dalton." Freezing, a hand on the doorknob, she stood with indecision, as she rocked her weight from foot to foot. "I shouldn't be out here at this time of night."

He waved away her protest and motioned for her to join him in the vacant rocking chair beside him. "I've always found listening to the land put itself to sleep a calming way to soothe my nerves before attempting to go to bed."

She sat in the chair, her weight shifted forward, her hands knotted together on her lap. "Although some of the creatures wake up at this time." As though to prove her point, a distant wolf howled.

He chuckled and nodded, pushing on a foot to put his chair back in motion. As he sat in quiet contemplation again, he noted her relaxing into the chair, until her head came to rest against the back of it, and she let out a quiet sigh of relief.

A soft breeze blew, and he saw her shiver. Fearing she would grab at that excuse to scurry back inside, he shucked his jacket, resting it over her like a blanket. In the faint light cast from a window, he saw shock and trepidation in her gaze. "No need to worry over a simple kindness."

She bit her lip a moment. "I've always found kindness never comes without expectations."

Settling again in his chair with a grunt of disgust, Dalton slapped his hands on the armrests. "Well, it does from me, Miss." He watched her out of the corner of his eye, as she snuggled into his jacket and sniffed at it. Flushing, he prayed it didn't stink too much of sweat and horse dung. "Why did you come outside?"

She seemed to shrink farther into his large jacket, causing him to note again how small she was. How delicate. He'd attempted to ignore how she had felt in his arms when she fainted. Soft. Voluptuous. Precious. Now she looked fragile, and he hated to think of anyone harming her.

"I forgot to open the window in my room today, and it's stuffy." She ducked her head. "And I was tired of listening to the men boast about conquests, as they played poker."

"Conquests?" he murmured. He shifted his chair, so he could better watch her, but he had given her the perfect armor, and now all he could see was her head, which she kept lowered. "I doubt the majority of them have danced with a woman, never mind kissed one." He smiled ruefully, as he met her startled gaze. "You must come to understand that most men will do anything to safeguard their pride."

Charlotte met his gaze for a long time. "I resent that their boasting is seen as something to be cheered. And they never have to worry about the women they harm."

"Talkin' about a woman from Laredo or Cheyenne isn't harmin' her, Miss," Dalton said. "Considerin' we all know the woman doesn't exist. It's what we do to pass the time and to forget we're still alone—and will probably always be alone."

She frowned, her cheeks a rosy red, as though embarrassed. "I'm surprised you're alone, Mr. Dalton."

He shrugged. "I wasn't meant to be. I married. Had a fine wife, who understood this life and who didn't mind it." He lowered his gaze and cleared his throat. "I've come to realize that the good times are never meant to last, Miss. It's why you have to enjoy those fleetin' moments of joy." When she stared at him in confusion, he murmured, "She died."

"Oh, I'm so sorry! In all the gossip, no one ever said

anything about ..." She bit her lip and shook her head. "I'm sorry."

"It was three years ago. I shouldn't let it ache as much as I do." He cleared his throat.

"You still miss her," she breathed, her voice filled with wonder and surprise.

He nodded, his gaze distant, as he focused on the faint outline of the chicken coop and the mountains in the distance. "Yes. I'll always miss her. She was my wife and my friend. When she died, my future died with her." He cleared his throat. "Mary died in childbirth and our baby with her."

Charlotte gasped, her hand clawing out from under the cover of his jacket to grasp at his. "Oh, Mr. Dalton. How tragic. I'm so sorry."

He shrugged, squeezing her hand once before releasing it. "Thank you, Miss." A barn owl hooted, and a cat yowled, as though in a fight. He cast a curious glance in her direction, attempting to decipher her mood in the faint light. "There's no need to be embarrassed, Miss. The men may jabber on, but they respect my privacy."

She sequestered her hand under his jacket again and let out a shaky sigh. After a long silence, she finally said, "I've thought only of myself. Of the disappointments I suffered. I haven't thought of the suffering of others. Or of what my actions could have done to others."

"*Hmm*," he murmured, as he settled into his chair, his hands clasped over his trim belly, as he tilted his head up to look at the stars. "After she died, I found I only had energy to focus on myself. If I'd tried to find compassion for anyone else, I would never have had the strength to recover. And then I would have been no good to anyone. Sometimes taking care of ourselves ain't selfish, Miss. It's a necessity."

"I hurt others," she said in a plaintive cry.

"Ah, that you did, Miss. Or you nearly did." He paused as

he saw her swipe at her cheeks, his fingers tightening on each other to remain clasped, as though reminding him that he had no right to reach out and to offer her comfort. "Seein' how everyone reacted tonight, Miss, you have no reason to fear that Slims and Miss Davina don't understand."

When he heard her attempt to stifle a sob, he swore under his breath. "Dammit," he muttered, as he eased from his chair and knelt in front of her. "It's all right, Miss. You're safe here with us. No one will harm you."

"You can't promise that!" she said, thumping him on his shoulder with an impatient smack. Her shoulders shook as pent-up sorrow finally erupted. "You say that now, but I know men. You're like little children with shiny toys. Someone else will come along and will interest you, and any concern for me will be forgotten." Her breath caught on a deeper sob, tears streaming from her eyes.

"Come here, darlin'," he murmured, settling on the wooden floor of the porch. He gave her hand a soft tug, and she tumbled forward of her own will into his arms and onto his lap. "Just as I remembered," he breathed. "Light as a feather." He maneuvered them so his back was to the wall, all the while cradling her on his lap.

Rather than encouraging her to quiet, he ran strong soothing strokes over her back and shoulders, murmuring soft words of comfort as she sobbed. He rocked them from side to side in a gentle motion, knowing it would calm her as it calmed him. When her sobs had quieted to gasping hitches of breath, he kissed the top of her head. "Ah, Lottie. When will you realize you will never be forgotten?"

She pressed her head into his chest, her hands clutching the rough cambric of his shirt. "I've never been memorable."

He chuckled, one hand holding her close, the other running softly over her head and silky hair. "Oh, I fear you're mistaken." When he attempted to ease her from his arms, she burrowed closer. With a contented sigh, he rested against the bunkhouse wall with her in his arms, his hands lazily stroking her back as she continued to recover from her crying fit.

"Why aren't you terrified of an emotional woman?" she whispered, her breath evoking a shiver as it tickled his neck.

"Why should I run from you, when you are showing me how you truly feel? To do so would be to dishonor you." He kissed her head again, as though unable to prevent showing her such tenderness. "To dishonor us."

Her head jerked up, and she peered at him with splotchy cheeks, reddened eyes, and a runny nose. "*Us?*"

"Tell me that you don't feel it," he whispered, "and I'll walk away and never bother you again. I'll be one more ranch hand who only comes to the kitchen for meals." He paused as her eyes widened. "Tell me." He winced as he saw her flinch, as his voice had emerged harder with a hint of desperation.

"Mr.—"

"It's Dalton, Miss. Just Dalton."

She bit her lip and then pushed back so she could stare at him. "I wish I could see you."

"Why?" His hand rose to continue to soothe her, as he felt nervous tremors move through her.

"To see if you are sincere." Yelping, she grunted as he dumped her on the floor and stood up.

"Sincere?" he hissed, keeping his voice low, so they wouldn't attract the interest of the other hands. "Sincere?" he asked again, unable to hide the hurt from his voice. "A blind woman could see truth from fiction, Lottie."

She pushed herself up, muttering her thanks as he helped her to rise, and he kept one hand on her waist as she listed from side to side. "That's the problem," she said, as she bowed her head. "I feel like I've been blind and dumb. I don't know up from down. I don't trust myself, Dalton."

He gave a grunt, but it was impossible to discern if it was of understanding or frustration. "What do you *feel*?"

She looked up at him, her face illuminated by moonbeams. "Can't you understand that the last thing I trust right now is how I feel? I was sorely betrayed by how I felt last fall."

"*I* am *not* him," he said in a low, clear voice, each word enunciated, as though shot from a pistol.

Her hands clutched at his arms, as though afraid he'd leave. "I know. And I know you've been good to me ever since I came back. And I remember how angry you were with Slims when you thought he'd acted dishonorably." She sniffled, shaking her head. "Don't you understand? I betrayed you too when I lied. When I refused to tell the full reason why I had returned."

He took a step closer, lowering his head, so they shared the same air. Looking deeply into her now-shadowed eyes, he said in a soft voice, "No, I don't see that. I see a strong remarkable woman who did everything in her power to survive." He nodded as two tears coursed down her cheeks, as she gaped at him in stunned wonder. "I see a beautiful woman who has the ability to leave the past where it belongs. If only she's strong enough to believe in the future."

"Dalton," she cried out. "That's not fair."

He ran a finger over her cheek, his jaw clenching, as though seeing her cry caused him physical pain. "Aye, it is, Miss. Take it from me. Leave the past where it belongs. Or you'll be condemned to live in it." He dropped his hands, picked up his discarded coat, and entered the bunkhouse, leaving her alone on the porch.

Once inside, he took an unsteady breath, waiting for regret to fill him for speaking so plainly to Charlotte. Instead

Dalton was filled with a sense of relief. Finally he had told her how he felt. He only prayed she felt the same.

∾

Charlotte watched the door close behind Dalton and sank to the rocking chair as his whispered heated words swirled around her. Clutching her hands to her chest, she shivered. How was she to be brave again, like he wished? How could she dare?

She took a deep breath and closed her eyes, as she thought about Dalton. His steady, quiet presence in her life. With a jolt, Charlotte realized she had come to expect he'd always be a part of her life. She stared into the dark in a daze. How had that happened in only a few short months?

Ever since her return to the ranch, he had acted as her shadow. Never threatening, always supportive and encouraging, he had been there whenever she needed help or a short pep talk. When the new hands had arrived, he'd ensured all treated her with respect.

Now she wondered if they had done so because they had understood she was Dalton's. Or because they believed she was as good as his. Rather than indignation or righteous anger, she continued to sit in a dumbfounded stupor as relief flooded her. Even when she was unaware, he had protected her from unsolicited advances from the new hands.

Charlotte considered all she did and did not know about Dalton. The other hands respected him, while Frederick and Slims seemed to consider him an integral member of their team. He was quiet and steadfast. Honest and seemed loyal. She knew nothing of his people and little about his past. Nor did she know how he reacted after too much liquor or when he was in an uncontrolled temper. What sort of man was he like then?

Although she had hurt him on the porch with her words when she questioned his honor and the veracity of his words, he had never lashed out at her. Would he lash out at her in the future?

Curiosity gnawed at her as she considered his first marriage. What had drawn him to the woman he called Mary? Would Charlotte have liked Mary? Charlotte shook her head at the inanity of her thoughts, pushing herself up with a groan, as her joints and muscles had stiffened in the cold.

She forced thoughts of romance and Dalton from her mind, easing the squeaking door open. She froze as she sensed she wasn't alone in the darkened hallway.

"There's no need to fear, Miss," Dalton said in a soft voice. "I wanted to ensure you returned to your room without problem." He paused, clearing his throat, his voice now barely louder than a soft summer breeze. "I wanted to ensure you didn't hate me."

She took a step inside, into the darkened hallway, her hand raised as though to stroke his cheek to soothe away the worry. She stilled the instinctual motion, her hand suspended in midair. "I could never," she whispered.

He clasped her hand, kissing the tips of her fingers. "You remained outside too long. You're freezing." Clamping his large warm hands around her frozen fingers, he used his body heat to thaw her cold hands.

Unthinkingly, she stepped forward into his arms. "You're like an oven." She pressed forward, shivering, as his arms wrapped tightly around her.

"Forgive me for taking my coat with me. It was callous." He kissed her head.

Pushing against his strong chest, she slid out of his arms. "No, it wasn't. It's yours, and you had every right to bring it inside." She stood now in the circle of his warmth but no longer touching him.

"Rest, Lottie," he murmured. "Your days are long." He ran a finger over her cheek. "Perhaps you'll dream of me as I do of you."

Her gaze flit to his, and she stood on her toes, kissing his cheek in a feather-soft caress, before dropping onto her heels and scurrying away. Once she'd shut and latched her door, she leaned against it, her cheeks flaming red. Why must she always act impulsively?

CHAPTER 4

Dalton entered the kitchen the following morning, after ensuring most of the other hands were already there. He felt uncomfortable and exposed after the previous night's events and didn't want to be alone with Charlotte right now. His left cheek burned, as though it were branded, where she had kissed it, and he knew he was being fanciful. He hadn't been fanciful since ...

Shaking his head, he grabbed a plate and served himself a generous portion of eggs, fried potatoes, bacon, and toast, before sitting at his usual place beside Shorty and across from Dixon. The other hands fanned out along the benches toward the door, away from the stove and Charlotte. As Dalton sipped at his coffee before he dug in, he realized he had claimed the seat closest to Charlotte, where he could watch for any prospective challenges to her.

With a sigh, he wolfed down his food, resolutely ignoring the inquisitive stares from two of his close friends. When Dixon kicked him in the shins, he glared at the young pup. "Don't start, Dix. You won't like how it ends."

Dixon flushed at the warning but sat back with a grumble. About ten years younger than Dalton, Dixon was no longer the green young man who had joined them years ago. However, he still saw the world with a youthful vitality that often left Dalton exhausted.

Shorty chuckled, munching on a piece of buttered toast. "You can try to ignore us, Dalt. But we'll badger the truth out of you sooner or later." With a wry smile he finished his meal and rose, murmuring his thanks to Charlotte, who remained overly preoccupied with polishing the stove so early in the morning. Dixon was on his heels.

Dalton ate the last few bites of his large breakfast, unable to remember what anything tasted like, and followed his friends. He cast a furtive glance over his shoulder, unable to hide a satisfied smile to see Charlotte staring at him with a wistful expression. He winked at her, a jaunty hitch to his stride, as he emerged outside to begin another long day in the saddle.

He saw Slims and Frederick walking in their direction and moved to meet them. "Boss, Slims," he said with a deferential nod. Like Slims, he wanted all the men on the ranch to always act in a respectful manner. Thus, even though Frederick and Slims were like family to him, he would always treat them with the respect they deserved during the time they worked together.

"You're staying here for the foreseeable future, Dalton," Frederick said. "You can help with the stalls and keep the ranch running."

"What?" Dalton sputtered. He looked from one to the other in horror at the thought of missing his time on the range, when everything was green with the promise of new life. Although he had readily agreed to forego riding out the previous few days, he had never expected to be stranded on the ranch for a long period of time. "I'm to muck out stalls, like a greenhorn?"

Frederick took off his hat, thwacking his thigh with it a few times, as he stared at the mountains in the distance. "Dammit, Dalton, I thought you'd want to stay here. To be near her. Am I reading the situation wrong?"

"She's on the ranch, Fred. She could spend her time with Miss Davina or Miss Sorcha. Miss Ingram wouldn't be alone then." Dalton closed his eyes, as he fought the sensation of being hemmed in.

"I can't imagine you'd miss a day of plannin' where a fence will go and figurin' out how to dig post holes and run wire," Slims said with a wry quirk of his lips. The giant of a man stared at his friend with fond understanding. "By the time we return tonight, you'll be thankful you weren't out with us."

Frederick nodded. "Aye, and most of the men won't be comin' back to the ranch each night. They'll take enough food so they can stay out for a few days or so." He watched his friend with a fierce intensity.

Dalton swore and paced a few steps away before returning. "I can't be away for days. During the day, yes, but not overnight."

Shorty, who had just sidled up to them with a cup of coffee in his hands, smiled as he held the coffee cup to his mouth. "And why would that be, Dalt? Could it be because you want to canoodle with a pretty woman at night?" He yelped as the coffee cup went flying, splattering the dark liquid all over his shirt.

"You talk about her with respect, Short," Dalton snapped.

Shorty held up his palms. "I ain't got a fight with you." He cast a furtive glance at Slims, who had lost his relaxed stance and stood straight, an alert gleam in his eyes, as he watched the two ranch hands. Shorty focused again on Dalton. "I thought you and she had finally stopped circlin' each other, after I saw you in the hallway last night."

39

Dalton sighed and rubbed at his forehead. "Sorry, Shorty," he muttered. "I hate what she suffered. And I hate that too many will consider her ..."

"Fair game," Slims said in a low, serious voice. "When word gets out what happened, too many will believe she's ripe for a repeat seduction, Dalt."

Dalton spun to stare out at the rangeland. A fierce desire filled him to ride out onto the range and to lose himself in days' worth of hard work, with nothing and no one to worry about except himself and his horse. He longed for the cloak of numbness he had shrouded himself in since he had lost Mary and their babe three years ago. However, that cloak had become tattered, as though devoured by a horde of hungry moths, and he now felt exposed and vulnerable. He had never wanted to feel this way again. Not about a woman who could leave him. Again.

He focused on the prairie, green and lush with the spring rains. A red-tailed hawk hovered in place as it caught site of prey, before swooping down. It rose again, with empty talons, to swoop and soar over the land. Dalton wished he were so unfettered and free and then closed his eyes, as he acknowledged he had lied to himself.

Considering the elation filling him last night after her innocent kiss on his cheek, he knew he couldn't leave. He couldn't merely hope that fate was kinder this time. Neither to him nor to her.

"I'll stay," he said. "Not because anything shameful happened last night," he said, as he opened his eyes and met the gazes of his friends. "But because you're right, Boss. I can't be away for days at a time. I'm needed here. And any work that must be done is good and honorable work."

Frederick nodded. "Aye," he said. "Tomorrow night expect to have the bunkhouse to yourself for a few nights. I'd expect I'll be the only one comin' back, as we work farther from the ranch. Sorcha'd skin me alive if I were to leave her with the twins overlong." He winked at them.

Slims and Frederick moved on to speak to the other men, leaving Dalton and Shorty alone. "Look, Short. I'm sorry," Dalton said, as he motioned at the man's shirt, now splattered with patches of drying coffee.

"It won't matter in an hour or two, when the whole thing will be sweat stained," Shorty said pragmatically. He studied the man he'd worked beside for over a decade. "What's the matter, Dalt? You're out of sorts, and that ain't like you." When Dalton remained quiet, Shorty nudged his side. "You'll have time alone with Miss Ingram, and you can see if you suit. Court her without all of us around." Shorty raised and lowered his eyebrows in a teasing manner.

Chuckling, Dalton huffed out a breath. "I suppose I could."

Shorty scowled at him, his hands on his waist, as he stared up at him. "Suppose? Suppose? Frederick is giving you the perfect opportunity to get to know her better, and you'll squander it? You have another chance, Dalt."

Dalton's smile froze, as he envisioned his future with Charlotte. At first, an incandescent joy filled him at the vision of Charlotte as his wife, at the secret smiles they'd share. Slowly the elation turned to dread, as he imagined her heavy with his child. He paled and swore, spinning away from Shorty's observant gaze.

"Dalt?" Shorty asked, gripping his arm. "What's the matter?"

"She'll die too," he rasped, as he ran a hand over his suddenly clammy forehead. "She'll die, and I'll have nothing but grief as a companion. I can't do that again."

Shorty looked to Slims, who approached them, shaking his head to keep his best friend silent. "You don't know that, Dalt."

41

Dalton nodded, his expression glassy and tormented, as though looking into the pits of hell. "But I do, Shorty."

Slims gripped his shoulders, giving him a swift shake that rattled his teeth. "What the hell's the matter with you?" His brown eyes gleamed with concern. "Are you ill?" At Dalton's silence, Slims looked to Shorty.

"Lovesick and terrified," Shorty murmured.

"Hell," Slims muttered, releasing Dalton. "I thought you'd want to stay here. Be close to her and have time to resolve whatever's between you." He waved his hand around. "It's plain as day to see somethin' more than friendship is there."

"Slims," Dalton said with a shake of his head. "I was a fool to believe I could begin again. That I had the right to forget Mary."

"That's a load of bull crap, and you know it," Slims said, leaning forward so he was eye to eye with his good friend. "Your Mary died due to misfortune. It had nothing to do with you. If you're too stupid to understand that and ungrateful enough not to grab at your chance at happiness now, there's nothin' I can say to change your mind." He looked to Shorty. "You can stay behind, Short, and keep the womenfolk safe."

"No," Dalton rasped, his blue eyes lit with determination. "I'm stayin'."

Slims nodded, a smile fighting to burst forth. "I thought you might. Come, Short. We're ridin' out." He nodded at Dalton, before heading back into the barn.

Shorty looked at Slims's retreating back before he spoke. "Slims has little patience for fear, since he and Davina faced theirs and found happiness." He paused. "You deserve more than a life in the bunkhouse, Dalt." He slapped him on his shoulder and sauntered off to saddle his horse.

Dalton walked through the barn to the paddock and opened the back gate so the men could ride directly out onto the range. After they had left, he watched their retreating forms and the puffs of dust kicked up by the horse's hooves. Already he struggled with an overwhelming desire to seek out Charlotte. To learn more about her. To spend time with her.

Instead he stood, staring out at the lush prairie in late May, knowing these days wouldn't last. Just like his days filled with delight with Mary, these were fleeting. Too soon the range would be baked brown, and the sun would be scorching hot, and few clouds would hold the promise of rain. He closed his eyes, forcing himself to think about Mary. Their life together. Their home filled with laughter and happiness. They'd had their disagreements and arguments but never anything that led to him sleeping in a chair.

His hand clenched around the wooden railing, as he remembered the night she died. The joy he'd felt at the start of her labor. The realization that something was wrong. Miss Helen's presence and then her frantic panic, which she tried so valiantly to hide from him as Mary bled to death. His attempt to be stoic. Philosophical.

He pounded his hand on the railing, grunting as splinters dug in deep. Lowering his head, tears leaked out, and he sobbed at the loss of his beloved wife and their babe. His shoulders heaved, as he mourned the dream of what he would never share with her. He wished he were brave enough to risk this pain for the love of Charlotte. He wished he believed what he had said to her the night before, that the past belonged in the past. With an acute clarity, he realized that some events would scar him forever.

The following night, Dalton shuffled a deck of old cards. He hadn't thought he'd long for the sounds of the men playing, the quiet mutters of distress as they received a poor hand, or the soft teasing as they heckled one another. Life in the bunkhouse hadn't changed much since he had first arrived over ten years ago, which was some comfort. Even though he found himself chafing against the monotony of the life, wishing the future held more for him, he feared he wouldn't have the courage to believe in his dreams again.

With a chagrined shake of his head, he laid out cards for a game of solitaire, his mind continuing to think through his current predicament, as he played the game. Although he had hoped he would be a father now, his wife by his side, he knew he should be thankful for the few years of happiness he'd had with Mary. Even though the acute ache of missing her had eased, the yearning for more remained.

Although a solitary man for the majority of his life, he'd never desired to live his life alone. After losing his family in the aftermath of the Civil War, he had dreamed of marrying a fine woman, like his mama, and having a half-dozen children. When he'd met Mary, he'd thought his dream would be fulfilled.

With a sigh, he cleared the game to shuffle the deck again to replay. Although he liked and admired Charlotte, he resented that her presence evoked memories he attempted to forget. Longings he wished he could ignore. As though conjuring her, he heard her call out to him from the kitchen. Setting aside the cards, he walked with a slight hitch in his gait, before loosening up after a few strides. "Yes, Miss?" he asked, as he entered the kitchen.

"Do you want a cup of coffee or tea?" She swiped at the

table, bending over and straining the buttons along the front of her dress.

Taking a deep breath and averting his gaze from her fetching form, he shook his head. "No, ma'am. Thank you. I've had enough for the day."

She rose, her cheeks a peony pink, while her hands fisted the rag. "Have I done something to offend you?" she whispered.

"No," he said, his gaze focused on the stove.

"Mr. Dalton, please," she whispered. "I ... I hoped," her voice faltered as it cracked. "I hoped we might be friends."

He had turned away from her, toward the kitchen window, cracked open to help cool the room after a long day of work, able to see her in the reflection of the glass. "We'll always be friends, Miss Charlotte." He cleared his throat. "Miss Ingram."

She tossed the rag onto the table and settled her hands on her hips, as she glared at him. "Why am I *Miss Ingram* again?" When he failed to meet her gaze, she stomped her foot on the ground. "What happened to the man from the other night? The one who wanted me to dream of him?"

At her plaintive voice, he sighed and rubbed at his forehead, before facing her. "He woke up." At her incredulous stare, he whispered, "Don't look at me like that. I've not played you false."

"How can you say that?" she asked in a tear-thickened voice. "You ... you made me believe you liked me."

He strode to her, gripping her shoulders, as he stared deeply into her eyes. "I do, Lottie," he said in a tormented voice. "God help me, I do. But I have no right. I'd ruin your life, and you deserve so much more than me."

Tears spilled onto her cheeks, and she shook her head. "I don't understand." She sniffled and stared valiantly into his gaze. "Don't you miss what you had? Don't you want that again?"

"I miss the promise of what could have been." His blue eyes blazed with torment and regret as he stared at her. "I never meant to hurt you, Lottie." He dropped his hands from her shoulders, backing up a step. "Forgive me," he rasped, clearing his throat. "I hope you have a good evening."

He spun on his heels, rushing out the bunkhouse door to stand on the porch. Although he yearned to race away, he was tethered to the place. By his loyalty to Frederick. And by his desire to keep her safe.

CHAPTER 5

Dalton sat on a comfortable chair in the bunkhouse a few nights later. Wood crackled in the potbellied stove, and he stretched his legs out in front of him, crossing them at the ankles. After a hard day of caring for the animals on the ranch, he enjoyed this quiet moment for introspection. However, he knew he was relaxed and reflective because Charlotte was humming in the kitchen. Knowing she was safe eased a worry that clung to him like a burr.

Taking a deep breath, he inhaled the subtle scent of lilacs and vanilla mixed with woodsmoke. A scent he would always associate with Charlotte. After opening one eye, he saw her hovering near the door to the large bunkhouse room. A room he'd never seen her enter. "Miss Ingram," he murmured, contentment and welcome redolent in his voice. "We're all alone. There's no reason not to join me."

She shifted from foot to foot, flushing as she saw him battling a smile at her girlish antics. "I'm certain it's not proper."

"Come," he soothed. "I promise, on all I hold dear, you're

safe." At her startled look, some of his ease evaporated, and he watched her with a penetrating gaze.

After a prolonged silence, she entered to perch on a chair near the stove. He watched as she reached out her hands, shivering, as though enjoying the warmth emitted from the stove on this cool May evening. "The weather changed," she whispered.

"If there's one thing that's constant here, it's that the weather will change," he said with a smile. Rather than attempt to soothe her into relaxing, which he sensed would only make her tenser, he eased back into his chair and acted as though she were barely present. "Thank you for supper. I could have heated a can of beans." He smiled as she sputtered in indignation, his eyes closing again as he relaxed.

"I was hired to cook. If there is one of you to cook for, I will do so."

He watched her through cracked eyelids. "Well, I appreciate it. Last cook was more interested in poker and liquor, so we never ate all that well. It's nice to have a decent meal after a hard day's work."

He watched as she relaxed into her chair, her hands easing their death grip on her skirts, until they played with a piece of string. He relished the quiet as he saw her gaze at the stove wistfully, her beautiful hair more red than blond in the soft lamplight.

"I shouldn't have been so concerned about my reputation," she said in a soft voice that barely carried to where he sat. "I'm foolish to think it still matters."

He uncrossed his legs, rocking them side to side as he continued to study her. "It's important to you, Miss. I wish I could say one mistake doesn't tarnish it forever, but we know the world isn't as forgiving to women as it is to men."

She nodded. "I've enjoyed my time here. I hate realizing I'll have to leave."

He sat up, his boot heels hitting the floor with a *clunk*, causing her to jolt. "Leave?" He shook his head. "Ain't no reason for you to leave, Miss. I've promised I'll act with propriety, and I will. None of the men will bother you."

She swiveled in her seat, so she faced him. "How can you be certain? I know you should be on the range right now. You shouldn't be doing menial tasks, like mucking out stalls and caring for the milk cows and tossing slop at pigs. You should be leading some of the men in whatever Mr. Tompkins needed you to do on the range."

He shook his head. "No, I do what Boss asks me to do. And the most important task was for me to remain here."

"Babysitting me!" she exclaimed, her hand slapping her thigh in agitation. "A woman you don't even esteem."

He eased from his chair and moved to crouch by hers, the lamplight limning his face, highlighting even more the sharp contours of his cheeks and nose. "No, I'm ensuring you are well. Ensuring no one arrived during the day while Fred's away to harm you or Miss Sorcha or Miss Davina. He entrusted your care to me, and I do not consider that a menial task, Miss Ingram."

She sighed with exasperation. "The truth remains, if I weren't here, you could do as you please."

He shook his head. "If you weren't here, I fear my heart would break." He flushed and cleared his throat at the inadvertent admission, rocking back on his heels to stand. "I beg your pardon."

"Why?" she demanded, rising. "Is it so terrible to believe you might have feelings for me?"

"No," he rasped, taking a step away from her. "Not at all." He stared at her in absolute bewilderment. "I'm being unfair to you, and I'm sorry. What do you see when you look at me?"

She frowned and bit her lip a moment, before shrugging,

as though she had nothing to lose by being honest. "A brave, decent, loyal man who I can trust."

He closed his eyes and let out a tortured sigh. "See? Right there's the problem. I'm not brave." He opened his eyes to meet her confused gaze, shaking his head in quiet entreaty for her to remain silent. "You don't understand what it was like. And I can't go through it again, Lottie." He closed his eyes a moment. "Forgive me. We all have a tendency to give each other nicknames."

She smiled, reaching forward to clasp his hand. Just when she was about to release it because he failed to react, he gave her hand a tight squeeze. "I like it. I've never been important enough to anyone for a nickname."

"I'm certain that's not true," he breathed, staring into her eyes for a long moment.

"Help me to understand," she whispered. "What was it like?"

He took a deep breath and motioned for her to sit again. He tugged his comfortable chair closer to hers, recapturing her hand to play with her fingers, while he sat with a distant gaze and spoke in a trancelike voice. "Have you ever seen someone die?" At her quick shake of her head, he shrugged. "I have. Far too many. When I came here, I thought I'd escaped senseless loss."

For many moments, the only sound in the room was that of the crackling wood in the stove and their quiet breathing. "The Tompkinses are good people. You've yet to meet Irene and Harold, Frederick's grandparents, but they're a pair of the kindest, most welcoming folks you'll ever meet. They seem to understand when you need a kick in your backside or a hearty meal or quiet companionship to ease your torment." He rubbed at the space between her thumb and her index finger, as though polishing it, the gentle motion soothing and intimate. "They never considered the ragtag group of men working for them as hired hands. We became family to them."

She watched him in wonder as he spoke. Intent on holding back all the questions wanting to burst forth, she instead listened, as he bowed his head and spoke in a soft hesitant voice.

"It was Irene who sent Mary to the ranch. Thought one of us would have the sense to see what a gem she was. She and Mr. Harold were livin' in town by then, workin' their café." He smiled, a momentary joy eclipsing the shadow of grief. "The other hands knew, somehow, that Mary was sweet on me. And I on her." He shrugged, his chagrined gaze flitting to hers. "We married in the fall after she arrived here, with Harold and Irene comin' out from town. We had the ceremony and a big bonfire, and we danced late into the night." His gaze flit around the room. "For a few years, I didn't live here but in a small cabin, near the one Slims and his wife share."

Charlotte nodded but remained quiet.

"I never knew such joy as the day she told me she was with child." He sighed, dropping her hand and rising to pace to the window to look out into the darkened night. "I should have learned that with such joy always comes an equal amount of sorrow."

"That's not true," she whispered. "Not all joy leads to pain."

He turned to stare at her, leaning his weight on the windowsill. "How can you believe otherwise?" He sighed as he saw her flinch at his words and the implied criticism held within. "Mary shouldn't have had trouble with the birth. She was a big strong woman. Well suited to life on a ranch. But the babe wouldn't turn. And Mary got so weak." His gaze was distant. "And I sat there, watching her die."

Charlotte shot up, her gaze defiant and pleading. "I'm

certain you did more than that." When he remained quiet, his expression distant, she cupped her hands around his cheeks, her fingers scraping along the fine stubble of his skin. "I know you would have fought for her in every way you knew how."

"Some things a man can't fight," he whispered. "Miss Helen was here. At the ranch. She did what she could, but ..." He shrugged.

Instinctively Charlotte moved forward, wrapping her arms around him and holding him close. She made soft soothing noises, as one does for an injured child. Gasping, as his arms banded around her with a fierce intensity, she didn't release him but held him even tighter. "*Shh*, Dalton. It's all right."

One hand rose to cup the back of his head, her fingers sifting through silky hair. She felt him shudder at her soft caress, and she murmured comforting words, as he struggled for control.

"Dammit," he rasped, as he backed away and turned from her. However, she saw the silver streaks down his cheeks, before he hid his grief from her. "Forgive me."

Although he would no longer face her, Charlotte continued to run her hands over his back in a calming pattern. "There's nothing to forgive," she murmured. "It's a relief to know not all men are devoid of emotions."

He looked over his shoulder at her, his gaze lit with a stormy amalgam of feelings: pain, longing, hope, despair. "Oh, I feel, Charlotte," he rasped. "God help me, I feel. I pray every night I never feel as much ever again."

Her hand dropped from his back, and she stepped away from him. "Oh, I see." She flushed and shook her head, as though having a silent conversation with herself. "Forgive me."

Dalton watched as she raced from the room, her skirts

whipping around her ankles and nearly tripping her in her eagerness to flee. "Damn," he muttered, bending forward to lean his palms against the windowsill. He wished he had the right to comfort her. He yearned to be the man who deserved to call her his. But he knew Charlotte's greatest risk didn't come from the faceless woman in town. It came from him.

The following day, Charlotte took advantage of the good weather to do washing. Without the men around, she had more free time in her day, and she relished her lighter duties. She admonished herself silently for she knew she was still receiving a generous salary, and she should offer to cook the meal for the big house too. However, she had never felt comfortable speaking with Sorcha and Davina. Although they had become more cordial to her during the past months, Charlotte had never forgotten that she had almost ruined a harmonious marriage.

She sighed, looking toward the mountains in the distance, before picking up a sheet to hang. She stood in front of the bunkhouse, where a few lines had been strung for drying clothes. The chickens clucked, and a rooster crowed in the coop to her left, while she heard horses neighing and Dalton whistling, while he worked in the horse barn to her right. A gust of wind caused the sheet to *thwack* her in the face, and she yelped, disgruntled and displeased with her work.

After wrestling the sheet onto the line and pinning it in place, she pinned the remaining clothes, calming with the sunshine, fresh air, and birdsong. Soon she was humming while she worked.

"Charlotte."

Yelping again, Charlotte spun to face the amused smiles of Sorcha and Davina. "Oh my," she gasped, as she stared at them. "I had no idea you were here. I mean, I knew you were on the ranch ..." She bit her tongue and stopped speaking, as they watched her with frank amusement. "Is there something I can do for you?"

"Aye," Sorcha said. "If ye're done hangin' yer laundry, I need ye in the big house."

Charlotte looked in the direction of the main ranch house and nodded, fighting dread. "Of course," she whispered. She dropped the last wooden pin she hadn't used into the basket at her feet and followed a chattering Sorcha and Davina. A lilac bush at the side of the house was in full bloom, its lacy purple blossoms sending its sweet scent into the breeze.

As they walked around to the back of the main house, a kitchen garden was in the middle of being planted, while the flower garden in front showed promise. Charlotte clambered up the steps to the porch behind them, coming to a halt at the sight of a table with three chairs, a pot of tea, and scones. "Forgive me. I didn't mean to intrude," she stammered.

"Ye are no'," Davina said with an exasperated roll of her eyes. "We wanted ye to join us. Sit." She had settled in one chair and Sorcha in another, leaving the middle chair free for Charlotte.

Charlotte studied them, suddenly sensing she was the main course. "Why?" she whispered, her hands clenched together at her waist.

Sorcha reached out a hand. "The wee beasts are takin' their nap, an' I have a few moments of rest. We want to ken ye better. I fear I've no' been as friendly as I'd like." Her gaze was filled with remorse. "Forgive me, Charlotte."

When Davina nodded her agreement to her cousin's statement, Charlotte shook her head in befuddlement. "How can you ask for forgiveness, when I'm the one who's wronged you?" She moved to the only empty chair and collapsed onto it. "I'm the one who nearly destroyed your marriage, Davina." When Davina laughed at her proclamation, Charlotte frowned with confusion.

"Nae, ye did no'. Ye caused me to have a few moments of doubt. But, in the end, ye helped make my marriage even stronger, for I showed Slims I trusted him, even without proof of his innocence." She looked at Charlotte with frank honesty. "I canna say I was no' angry with ye. But I kent somethin' was wrong from the first night I met ye. I've always regretted ye never desired my friendship."

Charlotte ducked her head, as Sorcha murmured her agreement to Davina's words. "I was pregnant with a married man's baby."

Sorcha took one of her hands and Davina the other. "Aye, ye were," Sorcha said. "But ye must forgive yerself, Charlotte. Ye were young an' naive an' dreamin' of a better future. He took advantage of yer innocence, an' I dinna mean the kind that occurs in the bedroom. I mean yer spirit an' heart an' sweetness."

Davina laughed at that. "Although Slims would say ye were no' sweet or kind when ye cooked for him an' Shorty at the far house last summer."

Charlotte flushed and shrugged. "I never liked Slims. I thought he was overbearing and bossy. But then, I suppose, that's how he must be as the foreman of a ranch."

"'Tis who he is," Davina said with a shrug, as though Charlotte's opinion of her husband were of no importance.

Sorcha smiled slyly. "Too bad Frederick did no' have the good sense to send Dalton to the far house last summer. Perhaps everythin' would have been a wee bit different now, aye?" Her eyes sparkled with mischief.

Charlotte flushed beet red at the implication. "I doubt it. Mr. Dalton is a kind man, but he has no interest in me." She watched as Davina and Sorcha shared an amused glance at her pronouncement.

"I ken ye've had yer disappointments, Charlotte, but I believe Dalton will no' be one of them," Davina said, hiding her smile behind her teacup.

Sorcha broke apart a scone and slathered on butter and then a little of last year's peach jam. "Ye ken his wife died?" At Charlotte's nod, Sorcha spoke in a low, reverent tone. "Ye ken that sort of loss would make a man cautious."

Flushing with indignation rather than embarrassment, Charlotte glared at Sorcha and then Davina. "Knowing what you do about him, why would you want me to be with him?" she demanded. "Why wouldn't you want a better woman for him?"

Davina frowned, and any merriment faded away as she met Charlotte's hurt gaze. "Ye ken I never meant to harm ye with my teasin', Charlotte." She clasped one of Charlotte's fisted hands, giving it a gentle squeeze. "I'm sorry ye've had such a difficult time, but dissatisfaction with that man from Butte should no' make ye believe ye are no' worthy of a fine man like Dalton. Only a lifetime of disappointment would."

Sorcha sighed when Charlotte continued to stare at the porch floor. "We hoped ye'd feel for him as he obviously feels for ye. An' that I'd finally have a reason to plan a weddin'. I've been denied attendin' too many recently."

Charlotte sputtered, her gaze flying to meet Sorcha's with incredulity. "You can't be serious. Dalton would never marry me."

Davina laughed. "That's the first time ye have no' called him *Mister*." She squeezed Charlotte's hand. "An', aye, he'd marry ye. Once he overcomes his fear that ye'll die on him, like everyone else he's ever cared about."

Shaking her head, Charlotte said, "No, he told me that he never wanted to feel strong emotions again. I will not force a man to care for me."

Sorcha laughed, pouring a tiny amount of tea into Charlotte's cup to warm it. "Oh, ye dinna ken men." She shrugged. "Although I dinna ken any woman who can say she truly understands them. But, with three brothers, I have an idea, aye?" She sobered. "My eldest brother, Cailean, is a fine man. He lost his wife and child, the way Dalton lost his Mary, an' it took Cail years to overcome the pain. He nearly lost his chance with Annabelle due to the fear of feelin' such pain again." Sorcha shrugged. "I've come to understand the greatest mistake I've ever made is to believe men do no' feel as much as we do. For they do. Their burden is they're no' good at expressin' it. An' they bluster an' act like fools with their friends rather than talk."

"*Truly* talk," Charlotte whispered.

"Aye," Davina said. "Come. Have a scone and some tea."

Sorcha cocked her head to one side and rose. "The wee beasts are awake." She scurried away inside to her twin children.

"Should we go?" Charlotte asked Davina.

"Nae, she'll bring them here, an' we can continue to enjoy our afternoon on the porch. We've earned a break from our hard work." Davina paused. "In all this, I assumed ye care for Dalton. Am I right?" When Charlotte nodded but flushed and ducked her head again, Davina whispered, "Why are ye embarrassed?"

"I'm ashamed," she whispered. "I allowed myself to be wooed by an unworthy man. I hurt others with my desperation."

Davina stroked a hand down the younger woman's arm. "We all make mistakes. An' I ken well enough the desire to be loved. To feel cherished. 'Tis a rare woman who could ignore that yearning."

"Why don't you despise me?" Charlotte rubbed at her cheeks, as she gazed at Davina in fascination.

Davina swiped at a strand of hair as blond as a sunbeam.

"I did. Ye ken I did. My love for my husband, our faith in each other, proved stronger than any feeling I could have for ye. An' I dinna say that to be cruel." She sighed as she stared at the rolling hills in the distance dotted with cattle. "I learned—with the help of good friends, family, and the love of a remarkable man—that I dinna need to be anything other than who I am to be worthy of love."

Charlotte stared at her in dumbfounded silence. "That's impossible. What we can do for others proves our worth."

Davina shook her head, her eyes shadowed by memories from her past. "Nae," she whispered. "I dinna agree. For too long, I tried to be what Da wished me to be. Biddable. Meek. I married a man who I didna love and was miserable."

Charlotte frowned at her. "You were brave enough to travel here alone."

Smiling, Davina nodded. "Aye. Brave and dumb enough no' to ken the danger of travelin' alone as a woman. I was lucky to always find chivalrous men who'd look out for me, an' I arrived unscathed." Her smile glowed brighter. "An' then I met Slims."

Nibbling at a scone, Charlotte whispered, as though she were admitting to robbing a bank, "I've never been brave." She flinched when Davina snorted and rolled her eyes. "Don't mock me."

"I will when ye're actin' like an *eejit* an' spoutin' utter nonsense." Davina looked to the noise at the door and Sorcha holding a wriggling child in each arm. After taking little Mairi in her arms and settling her on her lap, Davina said in a bemused voice to her cousin, "She doesna believe she's brave."

Sorcha frowned as she stared at Charlotte, before chuckling. "Ye've an odd notion about yerself, Charlotte." Sorcha patted at little Harold's bum, as he rested against her chest. He always had a much harder time waking up than his sister.

"Ye showed yer bravery when ye arrived here in February. Ye've shown it every day since ye demanded ye earn yer keep, rather than hidin' away in yer room." Sorcha was the picture of a contented woman, with a child on her shoulder, her eyes glowing with a deep joy. She softened her voice, as she gazed at the younger woman. "I dinna ken what it would feel like to suffer the betrayal ye did, but I hope ye ken the mistakes of the past, and the treachery of others, doesna preclude ye from finding yer own joy in the future."

"With Dalton," Charlotte whispered. When Davina and Sorcha nodded, Charlotte settled into her chair. "I don't know what to do. He … he opens up, and then he turns cold."

"He's afraid, aye?" Sorcha murmured, kissing Harold's head, as he made a sound of distress. "I ken a little about his life afore he lived on the ranch, an' it was a tryin' period." She shook her head, smiling wryly. "An', no, I willna tell ye what I ken. Ye need to learn all ye can from the man himself."

"Come. Drink more tea and have another scone. Relax an' enjoy the time when ye are no' so busy with all the men around. Too soon ye'll be worked off yer feet again," Davina said.

Charlotte relaxed into the chair, relishing her time with these generous women, as she suddenly realized she had friends.

CHAPTER 6

Charlotte sat in the kitchen that evening, nursing another cup of tea. The cool evening prevented her from sitting on the bunkhouse porch, and she had no desire to interrupt Dalton as he sat in introspective solitude in the main room of the bunkhouse. Too soon the men would return, and the room would be full of their chatter as they laughed, played poker, and told tall tales.

She smiled as she considered the conversation with Davina and Sorcha. After they had stopped pestering her about Dalton, Charlotte had enjoyed every moment with them. Their kinship and deep affection for each other had rubbed off on her, and any hesitation Charlotte had felt at being in their company had quickly faded. She had relished the sharing of worries and secrets, as they sipped too-strong cold tea, and she listened to them tell her fantastical tales about life on the Isle of Skye. Charlotte knew she'd never travel farther than Helena or Butte, if she were fortunate, but she enjoyed learning about the world.

Closing her eyes, she tried to envision what the glen where Sorcha and the MacKinnons were from was like, with the sea forming a harbor and the mountains in the background. According to Davina and Sorcha, faeries enjoyed playing with mere mortals and too often caused mischief in their lives. Sorcha didn't claim to have met one, although she seemed disgruntled to have been denied such an experience.

"What delights you?" Dalton murmured in a soft voice that felt like a caress.

Her eyes flew open, as she met his tender gaze. He stood, leaning against the doorjamb, with his arms crossed against his chest. Her breath caught at the depth of emotion in his gaze and her reaction to it. "Delight?" she asked, flummoxed. Her hands shook, as she attempted to raise her mug, so she lowered it again. "I was thinking about stories Miss Sorcha and Miss Davina told me. About their lives in Scotland."

He smiled. "I sat with Miss Sorcha after she broke her leg, when she was forced to spend the winter at the ranch with a bunch of hired hands for company. She told the best tales." His voice dropped to a near whisper. "I was worried about you today."

"Worried?" she asked, flushing as she realized she could barely string together a full sentence when he stared at her as he did.

"Aye," he murmured, as he pushed away from the doorway to walk with measured steps in her direction. "I came out of the barn and couldn't find you. Couldn't hear you singin'." He sat near her at the kitchen table, his hand reaching out so their fingers touched. "I ran around like a madman, lookin' for you."

"You did?" Her eyebrows rose, and she couldn't conceal the flash of delight in her eyes at his admission.

"Felt like a fool when I heard the three of you laughin' on the back porch."

Charlotte suddenly felt like a young woman with no sordid past and with a bright future. She dropped her chin, smiled at him, and flicked her gaze at him. "You should have joined us."

He chuckled, his fingers now gripping hers. "No one wanted a stinky ranch hand ruining the ladies' tea party."

"I wouldn't have mind." Her breaths came faster than usual, as though she had run from the big house, and she dropped her gaze, yanking her hand from his. "Forgive me. I can't imagine what you think of me."

"Charlotte?" He rested a hand on her arm to prevent her from bolting away from him. "What happened? I never would have flirted with you if I thought you weren't enjoying it."

Her breaths came out now in rapid succession, as though fighting panic rather than an overwhelming desire. She gasped, heaving in huge mouthfuls of air, but her alarm appeared to be increasing rather than abating. Her dulled gaze did not focus on him when he spoke.

"Dammit," he muttered. He stood, pulling her into his arms with a groan. He carried her through the silent bunkhouse to her nearby room, ducking under the low doorframe. He barely spared a glance at the Spartan room, with only a cot, a bureau, and a chair in a corner. After settling her on the cot, he released her, easing away.

"No," she gasped, "hold me." Tears leaked from her eyes, while her hands clutched at his gray cambric shirt. When he stared at her with hands fisted at his sides, sobs burst forth, and she rolled to her side, facing away from him. "Go!" she gasped through her tears.

"Dammit," he muttered again. After kicking off his boots, Dalton eased onto the bed, spooning her all along her back. He wrapped one arm around her waist, pulling her back tightly to his front, while his other hand rubbed her head. "You're all right, darlin'. *Shh*, love, don't cry so. You're not alone."

63

Heaving out a huge breath, Charlotte said in a stuttering gasp, "You didn't leave."

"Of course not."

"You're here because you felt a sense of duty."

He chuckled, his arm tightening around her waist. "I'm here because I hate to see you sad. I know you need to cry, Lottie, for you've suffered too much to keep it all inside. But you shouldn't have to cry alone. Not unless you want to."

"I deserve to be alone."

He sighed, his breath ruffling her fine red-blond hair. "What a bunch of horse dung. You don't deserve any such thing, darlin'. Except to be cherished and to be cared for."

She wriggled in his arms, until she had turned and could face him, her face splotchy from her grief. "I don't understand you. You want nothing to do with me."

"Ah, Lottie," he said with a tender smile, his hand swiping at her cheeks to smooth away the residual wetness on her cheeks. "You know that's not true. You know I want you." He stared deeply into her eyes. "But I should never have you."

"I don't understand." Two more tears tracked down her cheeks. "I understand your hesitancy because of who I am."

He tilted his head to the side, as though considering her words. "*Who you are?* Do you mean a beautiful, intelligent, brave, and kind woman? Is that what you mean? Or are you clinging to the lies spouted at you by that treacherous woman in Butte?"

Charlotte ducked her head. "I feel such guilt, such shame." When Dalton was patient, gifting her with his silence, rather than peppering her with questions or empty platitudes, she spoke in a halting voice. "I should have known better. I should have rebuffed that man's overtures." She sniffled. "And I should have known better than to chase him to Butte."

"How should you have known better, Lottie?" He cupped her cheek, his callused fingers stroking her silken skin. "You were desperate, and you wanted him to help you. You believed him to be a man of honor. And no man with an ounce of honor should have loved you and left you, like he did. Or thrown you to the wolves, like he did." He traced a finger over her eyebrows. "Proves he's the fool. And he will have his reckoning. I promise."

Her eyes filled with tears at his passionate vow, although none fell. "How can you be so good?" she whispered. "I brought my own pain on myself. I have no one but myself to blame."

"Ah, love, we all make mistakes in life. Some are costly. Others aren't. But all take a toll on our souls." His blue-eyed gaze bored into hers with a fiery intensity. "Why do you talk of me leaving? Why do you talk of your shame?"

Her lips quivered, as though attempting to hold back her words before she blurted out, "What must you think of me? A woman who throws her affection around so easily that—"

Dalton pressed his fingers to her lips and shook his head, silencing whatever nonsense she would have spouted. "No, Lottie. Don't speak poisonous lies to me. Don't lie to yourself." He took a deep breath, gazing deeply into her eyes. "You are not a woman who throws her affection around. If you were, you would have found any one of the hands acceptable as a protector during your time on the ranch."

She shook her head at the notion. "Never," she said around his fingers.

His eyes gleamed at her response. "Exactly. That's not the woman you are. You aren't calculating and conniving. Even in February, when you tried to trick Slims into marrying you, that was out of a desperate desire to survive." He smiled ruefully. "And we all know Warren was the one to come up with the plan. He's the conniving one."

She frowned. "I'd call him protective more than conniving."

Dalton ran the back of his fingers over her cheek, his brows furrowed, as he stared at her in confusion. "I don't understand his role in all this."

Charlotte shrugged. "One day you will." A few tears coursed down her cheek. "It won't matter. I have to find someone to marry me. To protect me. I discussed it today with Sorcha and Davina. It's the only way to keep me safe from Mrs. Coldwell."

A wry smile bloomed as he cupped her cheek. "Is that your idea of a marriage proposal?" He chuckled when she stiffened in his arms, then struggled to push herself over him to crawl from her cot. "No, Lottie, don't," he gasped. "Stay, please."

She shook and wrapped her arms around herself as best she could. "Why are you mocking me?"

"I'm not mocking you," he whispered, tenderness and a deep affection in his voice. He leaned forward, pressing his forehead against hers, as he closed his eyes. "Can you imagine the panic I felt today, when I thought something had happened to you?"

He opened his eyes, his gaze unmasked. "Every conceivable injury you could have suffered ran through my mind." He flushed and shook his head. "I realized something very important, Lottie." At her frown, his thumb played over the wrinkles in her brow. "I realized, by denying what we have out of fear of what might never happen, I was already living through my worst fear again. I was already losing you." He swallowed, speaking in a low voice. "And I can't do that. I can't lose you."

"What do you mean?"

"Marry me," he whispered. "Let me protect you, honor you, treasure you." When she stared at him in dumbfounded wonder, he breathed, "Please."

Her sherry-colored eyes shone with astonishment, as her

hand rose to clasp the side of his head. "Yes. Yes!" She gasped as he swooped forward, capturing her lips in a passionate kiss.

His hands sank into her lustrous hair, slipping pins from their moorings as the strands tumbled free. His hands held her head tightly, anchoring her in place for his deeply drugging kisses. He swallowed her gasp as he deepened their kiss, growling with pleasure as she pressed tighter into his embrace.

"We must stop," he breathed, peppering kisses over her brow, nose, cheeks, and chin. "I never want you to doubt how much I respect you. We have plenty of time for passion, darlin'."

She wriggled against him. "I wish the time was now," she murmured, earning a chuckle from him. She rested her head on his chest, curling against him with a contented sigh.

He ran his fingers over her back, closing his eyes, as he rested his head on the lumpy pillow. "This has to be the most uncomfortable cot I've ever had the misfortune of laying on."

She giggled. "I'm so tired at night after a hard day of work that I don't notice."

His hold on her tightened, and he murmured, "I promise we'll have more comfortable accommodations in our home."

She propped her head on her hands and peered at him intently. "We won't live here?"

"Hell no," he said and then flushed for swearing in front of her. "Pardon me." When she stroked a hand down his cheek, as though in forgiveness, he moved his head into her soft touch. "I want a home for the two of us. A place that is ours." His gaze clouded. "I fear the only cabin left is the one I shared with Mary."

"Will that be a problem?" she whispered.

"No," he said. "I swear it won't." He kissed her fingers and smiled. "Come. I promise I won't lead you down the road to temptation, but my cot's more comfortable." He winked at her, as she gaped at him in confusion. "Sleep in my arms tonight, darlin'. The men will be back tomorrow, and then I'll have to wait until our weddin' afore I can do more than steal a kiss."

With wide luminous eyes, she nodded. "Yes," she breathed. "I'd like that." She paused, as though gathering her courage. "I've never slept in a man's arms before."

He winked at her. "The first of many new adventures for us."

Dalton jerked awake, his dreams of holding his wife, Mary, melding with the present contentment of cradling a woman in his arms. Shaking his head, he gazed down at Charlotte, snuggled against his chest, sighing with delight. "It wasn't a dream," he whispered, running his fingertips over her brow.

In the faint dawn's light, her hair appeared darker, more red than blond. Any worry she carried seemed momentarily forgotten, as her expression was peaceful. Her soft breath tickled the sensitive skin of his neck. He gazed at her a long moment, imprinting the moment in his memory.

Closing his eyes, he sighed with a soul-deep contentment. He had learned to accept these perfect moments of peace and to treasure them. For he never knew when he would be gifted with another. He prayed his life with Lottie would be filled with such moments, but he knew there were no guarantees. Too much remained that he did not know and did not understand.

When she stiffened, he slitted his eyes open to gaze at her. "Hello, love," he murmured, kissing the top of her head. "No need to panic. No one is here but you and me."

Charlotte pressed up, her elbows digging into his belly, earning a grunt of protest. "What was I thinking? This isn't proper. What will they think?"

He cupped her head, staring deeply into her panic-filled eyes, instantly mourning the loss of their peaceful interlude and the return of her worries. His thumb traced the furrow between her brows. "Love, calm down. We've done nothing wrong. If my memory serves, we're engaged."

"I'm proving everyone right!" Charlotte cried out. "I jump into bed without a moment's thought …" She bit her lip, swallowing what more she would have said when noting the anger and disappointment in his gaze.

"That can't be true," he whispered. "For you didn't jump into any bed that was offered to you. You waited for me. And, for that, I will always be infinitely grateful."

"I slept in your arms," she muttered.

Shaking his head in confusion, he whispered, "Weren't you comfortable?" At her nod, he urged her down to rest against him. "You're all mixed up, my Lottie. Why shouldn't you enjoy resting in my arms?" When she remained quiet, he ran his hands over her back in a soothing manner, sighing with relief when she settled against him. He felt the tension ease from her, and he wondered if she would slip back into sleep.

"I've never had this," she said in such a low voice that he almost didn't hear her. "This sense of feeling adored." She pressed her head into his neck, breathing deeply of his musky scent and a hint of pine from the soap from his hasty wash the night before. "I get prickly when I feel trapped."

"I never want you to feel trapped, Lottie. But I will protect you. And cherish you." His fingers played through the long tresses of her hair. "I hope you are able to see the difference."

She pressed up again, her sherry-colored eyes filled with chagrin. "I may need your help to teach me the difference."

"Oh, love," he murmured, as he kissed her head. "Gladly."

D alton stood in the kitchen doorway a little later that morning, watching as she moved from the stove to the sink to the table in a perfectly synchronized dance. He had forgotten how much joy he could feel from the simple activities that occurred each day. "Hello, love," he murmured, smiling as she jumped at his gentle sleepy voice.

"Dalton," she gasped, as she spun to face him, an untroubled look in her gaze.

He froze as it was the first time he'd seen her so at ease, with no evidence of any worry. "You're finally at peace." He walked to her, as though in a trance, mesmerized by the radiant pleasure in her expression. Cupping her cheeks, he scraped his thumbs over her skin.

She nodded, her eyes shining. "Yes. You want me. Not just for passion."

He shook his head and then nodded, before grumbling as she laughed. "No. Yes. I want you, but not only for the passion I know we'll share. I want the conversations and the laughter too. My soul calls out for times when I can hold you in my arms and can feel as though everything is right in the world, simply because you are beside me."

She pushed a lock of hair back as she gazed deeply into his eyes. "It's like you said when you talked about …" She paused as she broke off, as though uncertain if she should speak his dead wife's name.

"*Mary*," he coaxed. "Her name was Mary, and I—we—should speak of her. To relegate her to silence is to dishonor her and her memory."

Charlotte nodded, taking a deep breath. "When you spoke of Mary, you said she was your friend as well as your ..." She broke off again, flushing.

"As well as my lover," he said with an adoring smile. "Yes, she was. As I hope you will be. I want more than a woman to warm by bed and to cook meals and to wash clothes." He stiffened as her eyes filled with tears. "I can do all that stuff for myself." He paused as she stared at him with an expression he couldn't read. "I hope you want more too, Lottie."

She nodded, pressing into his embrace. "Of course I do. You'll have to be patient with me. I don't have much experience with that sort of relationship." She shuddered, as his arms wrapped around her, and he kissed the top of her head. "I feel so safe with you," she breathed.

"Good," he whispered. He rocked them gently side to side as a rooster crowed, and the room brightened with the rising sun.

At the amused chuckle behind them, they sprang apart. He pushed Charlotte behind him, so as to protect her, while he glared at the person interrupting their quiet morning.

"I should have kent better than to interrupt," Davina said with a chagrined smile, her eyes dancing with merriment.

"Miss Davina," Dalton said, as he heaved out a relieved breath. Charlotte moved to his side, and he relaxed when she dropped her hand to clasp his fingers in hers. "I ... Is there somethin' you need?"

She shook her head. "Nae, I feared ye were ill when I did no' smell breakfast cookin' this mornin', as I made my way to the big house. I'm sorry now to have interrupted ye."

Dalton rubbed his grumbling stomach at the mention of breakfast, and Charlotte moved away to pour a cup of coffee from the pot. She thrust the cup at him, nearly scalding his hand, as drops of it sloshed over the side.

"I'll start it right away. I slept late. It was selfish and

foolish of me," she stammered, as she wrapped an apron over her blue gingham dress. "I …"

Dalton set down the full cup of coffee, gripping her arms to still her frantic movements about the kitchen. "Lottie," he murmured in a soft direct voice. "Ain't nothin' selfish about sleepin' a little longer when you're as exhausted as you were." He ignored Davina standing behind him. "I'll survive if I don't eat breakfast."

"I dinna ken if I will," Davina said in a cheery voice. "Why do ye no' join Sorcha an' me at the big house? We always have food for twenty." Her retreating footsteps were heard. "We'll expect ye in a few minutes, aye?"

"Aye!" Dalton called out, waiting until he heard her softly close the outer door. "Lottie, what's the matter?" He held a firm grip on her shoulders, when she would have raced after Davina.

She looked to the stove with a deep longing. "I earn my worth by the work I do. I must go help Miss Sorcha and Miss Davina."

He shook his head, his expression fierce as he looked at her. "No. Not until I hope you understand something." He paused and took a deep breath. "You earn your worth by being who you are, darlin'. I don't care what you do, as long as you are honest and loyal."

She gazed at him in bewilderment. "I don't understand."

"If you like to cook, cook. If you like to sew, then sew." He pursed his lips in frustration, as though attempting to find the words he needed to express himself. "I've lived many years alone, Lottie. I know how to cook and to clean after myself and to wash my clothes. I can sew good enough for what I need done. I don't need a maid or a cook or a wash-woman." He waited as she watched him with wide-eyed fear. "I want you. I want to share my life with you." He rubbed at her shoulders. "Can you understand the difference?"

A tear coursed down her cheek, and he leaned forward, kissing it away. "I'd take your sorrow and make it mine, if I could."

Charlotte ran a hand through his silky hair, still damp from his hasty wash before breakfast. "I comprehend the words, Dalton, but I don't understand." She backed away and pressed a hand to her heart. "In here. I've never been valued for anything other than what I could offer."

His gaze filled with sorrowful regret, as he cupped her cheeks. "I know, Lottie, and I'm so sorry. I'm sorry no one saw you as the magnificent woman you are. But don't let their failings limit you."

She sighed, pressing herself into him again. "I'll try, Dalton. I promise."

He let out a sigh of relief as he held her close. "Come, love. If we don't arrive for breakfast soon, Sorcha will traipse over here, and then we'll never live it down. She'll invent all sorts of tales to tell Frederick." He leaned back and winked at Charlotte, as he dropped his hand to clasp hers.

They walked, hand in hand, enjoying the early morning as the day brightened and as the birds sang. "We're too late to see the pink sunrise over the mountains. It's magical to see the clouds change color as the sun rises," he murmured. He led her up the side entrance into the kitchen, scraping his boots as he entered. In the large kitchen, he saw Davina setting out a platter of eggs, bacon, and fried potatoes, while Sorcha buttered bread.

"The twins?" Dalton asked, as he nodded his hello to the women.

"An' a good mornin' to ye," Sorcha said with a wry smile. "They're still asleep, although I ken they'll wake soon." Her assessing gaze roved over the pair, taking in their clasped hands. "I ken well enough ye are passin' yer time in a worthwhile fashion."

73

"Miss Sorcha," Dalton said, a warning note in his voice.

She shared a smile with Davina. "Ye ken I only ever want ye to be happy, Dalton." She motioned for them to sit at the large table. When they sat across from her and Davina, who had settled beside Sorcha, Sorcha continued to watch them closely. "Are ye playin' her false?" At his outraged grunt, Sorcha gave a satisfied nod. "What do ye have planned?"

Dalton served himself a large portion of eggs, then held the platter for Charlotte, before setting it down. At Charlotte's subtle nod, he said, "We plan to marry."

Davina squealed with delight, rising to hug Charlotte and Dalton, nearly jumping with joy. "Oh, Sorcha, we couldna have planned this better."

"You didn't plan anything," Charlotte protested.

Sorcha shrugged, as she hugged the two of them and retook her seat. "A wee nudge. That's what ye needed. I kent the man would be mad with worry lookin' for ye. An' I hoped he'd come to his senses." She smiled with understanding, as she saw Dalton duck his head. "Ye've mourned long enough, Dalton."

He nodded, his gaze averted. "I know." He played with his spoon, turning it over and over again. He stilled his movements when Charlotte rested her hand on top of his. He cast a grateful look in her direction. "I know," he repeated in a softer voice.

Sorcha sighed at the sight of them. "Ah, I remember this time of young love, when I thought Frederick hung the moon."

"Ye still do," Davina said, as she nudged her cousin with her shoulder.

Giggling, Sorcha nodded. "Aye, I do." Answering Dalton's unspoken question, she said, "He spent the night with the men last night on the range. They'll all return tonight, in need of baths and a huge meal."

"Slims will be delighted that ye came to yer senses," Davina said. "When will ye marry?"

Sorcha gasped, dropping her piece of toast onto her plate, as she spun to face Davina and then Charlotte and Dalton, her hands in front of her, as though helping them to envision her wonderful idea. "I ken when ye should marry!"

"Tonight?" Dalton asked in a hopeful voice.

"Nae, ye impatient man," Sorcha said with a roll of her eyes, earning a giggle from Charlotte. Sorcha fought a smile as she saw Dalton squeeze Charlotte's hand. "Nae, ye should marry at the Founders' Dance."

"The dance?" Charlotte breathed, her happiness extinguished as quickly as a fire under a bucket of water. "But she's in town. And she means me harm."

"Nae," Sorcha said. "She willna have a chance to harm ye. I promise," Sorcha said. "Ye'll have us an' the MacKinnons an' all our extended family around ye. We're better than any army." She sobered as she met Dalton's concerned gaze. "An' ye ken 'twould help to marry in front of the preacher, in a planned ceremony, rather than earn infamy by marryin' in haste again."

"Again?" Charlotte whispered.

"Nae, no' Dalton," Davina said, "but everyone associated with the MacKinnons tends to marry in a scandalous manner or without the preacher present. This way, ye'll have nae reason for the townsfolk to ever question the validity of your union."

"Why should they care?" Charlotte asked.

Sorcha rolled her eyes before chomping on a bite of bacon. After a moment, she swallowed and said, "Oh, they care, a wee bit too much, about anythin' a MacKinnon or a MacKinnon associate does. This will save ye heartache. I promise ye."

Wriggling her eyebrows at Charlotte, Davina said, "And it

will give most of us an excuse to go to town for the dance." They knew a few of the hands would need to remain to care for the horses and other livestock while they were away.

"An' I'm no' missin' another weddin'!" Sorcha proclaimed. Staring at the betrothed couple, she asked, "What do ye think? Do ye want to marry in a little over a week?"

Dalton frowned and shook his head, before he sensed Charlotte tensing beside him. "No!" he gasped, gripping her hand and turning to face her. "That's not what I meant. I want to marry you now. Waiting another week will seem like forever."

She studied his expression, as though searching for deception. When she saw none, she relaxed and began to eat her breakfast again.

"Where will ye live?" Davina asked, her gaze moving between the three other occupants in the room. As a stilted silence descended, she demanded, "What do I no' ken?"

"Uh, we'll live in the empty cabin by you and Slims," Dalton said with a determined nod.

"Are ye sure?" Sorcha asked. She sighed when she heard the first cry from one of the twins, rising to calm them and to fetch them.

"Why should ye no' live there?" Davina asked, as she took a sip of tea. She studied them over her teacup, her blond hair tied back in a braid.

Flushing, Dalton spoke in a soft voice. "I lived there with my first wife. Before she died in childbirth."

"Oh," Davina breathed. "I beg yer pardon. I didna mean to cause ye sufferin'." She reached out a hand to pat their joined hands. "I ken well enough what it is to return to a place where a ghost lurks."

Dalton huffed out a breath and shook his head in exasperation. "No ghost lives there, Davina."

"Ye never ken," she murmured. "I felt like my first

husband haunted my every step until I fled our home. 'Twas the first time in years I felt I could take a full breath." She took one now, as though to show she could breathe well, causing Charlotte to giggle. "No' all fear is rational."

"No, it isn't," Dalton said. "But it's a good solid cabin, just like the one you live in. It'll be a good home for us."

Sorcha arrived with the twins, handing Mairi to Charlotte to cuddle, as Davina continued to eat her breakfast. Sorcha walked around the kitchen, rocking a fussy little Harold as he woke up. "The wee man never seems to understand life will be full of surprises and adventures once he awakens." She ran a loving hand down his back.

Charlotte snared Dalton's attention as she *coo*ed and cuddled Mairi. Charlotte laughed as she arched her head back, keeping the curious girl from pulling at her hair, and settled her on her lap, facing the table, where Mairi proceeded to pound on it with a broad smile. He felt his breath catch at the absolute joy in her gaze as she cradled Mairi on her lap, and a fierce desire filled him to share daily moments just like this with her. He prayed fate would be more generous this time.

CHAPTER 7

The next day Dalton worked in the barn, giving each horse its portion of oats. He paused in front of one stall to scratch behind Boots's ears. Boots was Frederick's favorite horse and received an unfair amount of attention from all the hands due to that fact. She was also friendly and beautiful and never mean. "You like that, don't you, girl?" he murmured.

"Tell me a woman who doesn't like a little pamperin'," Frederick said, as he sidled up next to his friend. He slung his arms over the railing before patting Boots on her muzzle. "Hi, girl," he murmured. "You earned your rest." He looked around his prized horse barn with pride. "I'm sure Slims told you, but we got a fair amount of work done the past week. Although I expect we'll have to do more out near the Henderson homestead."

"Aye, but that's not urgent. I'd expect it'd be more important to keep the cattle closer to where you plan on spendin' the winter." He saw Frederick nod, although his gaze was distant.

"I'm not used to this kind of ranching," Frederick

muttered. "I liked it when it was all open and when the cattle ranged here and there, with a spring and a fall roundup. Now the land's marred by our fences, and a man can't roam as he's meant to."

"Free," Dalton said, as he finished working his way down the long row of stalls, murmuring sweet words to each horse.

"Aye. Free." Frederick sighed. "I can't imagine my brothers being willin' to settle down here, Dalt. And they won't be able 'to run many more herds north. Not with the way things are. It's almost 1890, for heaven's sake!"

Dalton chuckled. "Your brothers can figure out what they'll do. And they're smart enough to know the runnin' of the ranch is yours. There'd be a mutiny on their hands if they tried to change that."

Muttering his appreciation at Dalton's show of loyalty, Frederick gave a final pat to Boots, although he continued to lean against the stall of his trusted horse.

Dalton noticed Frederick remained beside Boots, although he felt Frederick watching him. Finally he asked, "What is it, Boss?"

"I heard you plan to marry," Frederick said. "I'd hoped you'd tell me yourself."

Dalton sighed and set down the bucket of oats in the feed room, before walking toward Frederick. He plucked a piece of hay from the stacks in the barn and twirled it between his thumb and finger. "I figured Sorcha would enjoy tellin' the tale about our breakfast together yesterday mornin'."

Chuckling, Frederick joined his friend. "Aye, she did. However, it wasn't her story to tell. What troubles you?"

Dalton shrugged. "I care for her, Fred. You know I do."

"You've been mooning after her for months."

Dalton chuckled and nodded. "Yeah, that about sums it up. But I never planned to marry again. And she's young. She could do better than an old cowpoke like me." He ran a hand through his brown hair with no hint of gray.

Staring at Dalton with sharp intelligent eyes, Frederick shook his head. "There's more to it than that. There's more to it than your fear, even though I understand that would seem insurmountable."

"What more is she hiding? Why won't she talk about Warren's role in all this?" Dalton asked.

Frederick nodded. "I see." He paused. "You asked her to marry? You weren't coerced?" When Dalton rolled his eyes and shook his head, Frederick paced away and then back to him. "Fine. We go to town as planned and talk to the preacher. However, if you're not satisfied with what Warren tells you beforehand, don't marry her."

Sputtering, Dalton gaped at Frederick. "I can't abandon her at the altar. That would be worse than … worse than lettin' just any old cowpoke have her." He waved in the direction of the bunkhouse and the numerous men there.

"Aye, but a life forged on lies would be far more cruel. For you. And you're family, Dalt. I won't have my family harmed." Frederick gripped his shoulder and then slipped from the barn, leaving Dalton deep in thought.

Dalton sat on the front porch, listening to Charlotte work in the kitchen. Now that he and Charlotte were engaged, he knew no one would comment on him remaining in the kitchen after dinner. Heck, none but Shorty or Slims would have dared comment before he was engaged. However, he needed a little time to consider what he wanted to do.

With a long sigh, he tilted his head back and stared at the darkening sky and the first glimmer of stars. This time of year, it would take a while before the sky darkened enough for him to fully enjoy the brilliant splendor of the night sky. His focus returned to the conversation he'd had with Frederick and the restless feeling it evoked.

Now that he'd asked Charlotte to marry him, their union was all he could think about. The small intimacies that came with marriage. Brushing out her hair. Holding her hand under the table, as the men chattered around them. Sharing a secret look that only they understood. Evoking a smile or a laugh. Small moments that created a life to be cherished. None of it would be possible if there were secrets between them.

The door squeaked open, and Dalton met Charlotte's hesitant smile. "Hello, love," he murmured, holding out his hand for her. Rather than easing her into her own chair, he tugged her to him, so she'd settle on his lap and in his arms. "You're not heavy."

Soon she had relaxed in his embrace, her head coming to rest on his shoulder, her arms wrapped loosely around his neck.

"How was your day?"

"Wonderful," she whispered. "I spent a good portion of it with Davina and Sorcha. They're sewing me a wedding dress." She ran her hands over his strong shoulders, frowning at the tenseness she detected. "What's the matter?" She nuzzled the side of his neck, earning a shiver.

Kissing the top of her head, he closed his eyes. "You're too perceptive." He ran a soothing hand down her back. "It has nothing to do with work. I spoke with Frederick today." He frowned when he felt her tense.

"He doesn't believe we should marry." When he remained quiet a breath too long, she rasped, "He knows you could do better than me and advised against you making such a foolish decision."

A quivering tension ran through her, and he wrapped his arms tighter around her. "No. That's not how Boss is, and I'd think you'd know that by now. Besides, Sorcha'd knock him on top of his head with a skillet if he interfered with the wedding she believes she brought about." When Charlotte giggled, he let out a sigh of relief. "No, Lottie, he brought up another concern. One I've tried to ignore."

Wriggling until she had maneuvered so she could see his face, she whispered, "What?"

"I can't marry you—"

She thrust out her elbow, hitting him in his neck and nearly cutting off his airflow. While he gasped for air, she heaved herself off him.

"Lottie, damn it," he gasped, as he rose, catching her as his arm snaked out to wrap around her waist and to yank her back against him. "Stop fighting me." Dalton coughed a few times, holding her close. "Listen," he pleaded into her hair that had come loose from its braid. "Please, Lottie, listen."

"I have no choice because you hold me prisoner here," she snapped in a petulant tone.

"Prisoner?" He loosened his hold and took a step away. "If that's how you feel, please leave." He backed up again, until he was steps away from her, and it felt as though an impenetrable chasm was between them.

She looked over her shoulder and froze, her gaze meeting his tortured one. "Dalton," she pleaded. "Don't play with me."

"I'm not. I don't understand what just happened." His blue eyes shone with frustrated regret. "One moment I was holding you in my arms. The next you were beating me to get away."

"You said you didn't want to marry me." Her voice came out in a plaintive wail, her eyes glowing with unshed tears.

"No, I didn't." He closed his eyes a moment, as though praying for peace. "You didn't let me finish what I was going to say." He waited to see if she would bolt, but she remained in front of him. In a gentle voice, he said, "I can't marry you, Lottie, if there are secrets between us." He paused, taking a cautious step toward her. "I can't marry you not knowing why Warren sent you here. I can't protect you and our family if I don't fully understand."

She let out a deep breath and nodded. "I can't tell you." She held up a hand, pleading for understanding. "It's not my secret to tell. Not wholly. Will you trust me, please?" Her voice broke on the *please*, and she lowered her head, as though believing she wasn't worth such emotion.

"Lottie," he breathed in a soothing voice.

"Trust me until we can talk with Warren? Together?" She took a deep breath and met his gaze.

"Of course." He stroked the backs of his fingers over her cheeks. "Knowing you are willing to share this with me eases my concern, Lottie." He took a deep breath. "If Warren doesn't want to tell me, I'll need you to choose me, love."

She nodded. "I know. I will. But only Warren can tell you these things. Things I still don't fully understand. If he's willing to talk with us …" She shrugged.

"Whatever he says will ensure I'm better able to protect you and to alleviate your fears." At her breathed, "Yes," he pulled her close, burying his face in her silky hair. "Thank you for trusting me, Lottie." He felt her shudder and feared she was crying. "I promise I won't betray it."

She gripped his back, holding him tight. "You have it backward, Dalton. You trust me, which is such a miracle."

"Ah, love, that's what marriage is all about."

Davina arrived at the bunkhouse early that Saturday, almost a week before they were to head to town for the Founders' Dance. She poked her head into the kitchen and smiled at Charlotte. "He did no' tell ye, did he?" she asked, as she tied an apron around her waist.

At the sound of her voice, Charlotte jumped, a skillet rattling on the stove. "Oh, you scared me." She held a hand to her waist and stared at Davina with wide eyes. "Please, don't sneak up on me."

Nodding, Davina walked into the room with an even step. "Aye, I'm sorry. I remember you nearly stabbin' Dalton recently. I should have kent better." Her gaze was filled with remorse. "I promise. I willna ever sneak up on ye again. I'll make enough noise to sound like a herd of buffalo." She smiled when Charlotte giggled. "Come. Let me help ye."

Charlotte stared at her quizzically. "I don't understand. I've been making breakfast for the men for months. Why should I need help now?"

"Well, ye never were engaged to one of 'em afore," she said with a wink. "An' I'm no' goin' to ruin the surprise."

Standing with a befuddled look on her face, Charlotte held a spatula in one hand and the other fisted on her hip. "Surprise?"

Dalton entered the kitchen, his brown hair wet from a recent dousing and his blue cambric shirt enhancing the blue of his eyes. "Hello, love," he murmured, smiling his thanks as he accepted the cup of coffee she gave him. "I hoped we'd have time together today. Davina is going to help here, while we are away for a few hours."

"Away?" Charlotte asked, paling. "Why would we leave?" A subtle tremor moved through her.

Dalton ignored Davina, who had taken over the preparations for breakfast, setting aside his coffee cup to gently clasp

Charlotte's shoulders. "Lottie?" he murmured, bending forward, his sole focus on her. "What's the matter?"

"I'm safe here," she gasped out. "In the bunkhouse. In the kitchen. I'm safe." She waved an arm out, indicating the rangeland and the world outside the ranch. "I'm not out there."

Dalton ran a thumb over her cheek, waiting for her panicked breaths to calm. He stared deeply into her beautiful sherry-colored eyes, his calm and quiet acceptance of her panic soothing her. When she relaxed, he murmured, "I will be with you. I promise nothing will happen. But, if you prefer to remain here, we can have our picnic on the kitchen floor." He smiled as she was unable to fight a startled chuckle of laughter. "Or in one of the nearby fields."

She gazed deeply into his kind and understanding gaze. "What did you envision?"

He smiled. "The wildflowers are starting to bloom, and I wanted to take you to one of my favorite spots. A place I've only ever gone alone. To share it with you." He caressed her cheek again. "It's about a half-hour ride, maybe a little more, from here."

Stepping forward, she pressed into his chest. "Yes, I'll go there with you," she breathed. "I want to be brave."

He chuckled. "You are, Lottie. You always have been."

A few hours later, he rode beside Charlotte with the ranch behind them. Rather than head toward the mountains, he rode toward the hills in the distance. Soon all they heard was the sound of the breeze through the long grass and the birds serenading them. He grinned at her, his smile deepening to see her unfettered delight as she looked around the rangeland. After the snowmelt and the spring rains, the rangeland and surrounding hills were a deep green. Trees blossomed; flowers bloomed, and birds busily built nests.

"It's so beautiful," she breathed.

He shifted in his saddle, as he looked around with pleasure and pride. He would always feel grateful that he was a trusted member of Frederick's crew. "Yes. This is one of my favorite times of the year. These are nurturing times. There's plenty of grass for the cattle, and the worry about a drought is still a ways off."

"Would you ever consider raising sheep?" she asked, smiling as she saw him scowl at her question.

"Cattlemen don't have much use for sheep," he said with a shake of his head. "Although I have heard Miss Sorcha badgering Boss about getting a small herd. She'd like to raise her own source of wool." He shook his head, as though that were a blasphemous idea.

"Who owns this land?" she asked as she looked over the wide expanse of the valley. Cattle dotted the distant rangeland.

"Boss and his family," Dalton said. "They own almost everything you can see." He motioned to a spot in the distance. "Except that other ranch house over there." When she nodded at a farmhouse far away from them, he said, "The Evers family. They're our closest neighbors. A good half hour ride away. Maybe a bit more."

Charlotte looked around the largely empty expanse of land. "Why do they need so much land?"

Dalton shifted in his saddle. "Do you recall the fierce winter from a few years ago?" At her nod, he said, "Well, we —Boss—almost lost it all. Thought he'd have to sell up and to find some other work. Damn near broke his heart. He worried about his marriage, about not being able to provide for his wife, his children." He sighed as he shook his head.

"Shorty saved everything by ridin' in with a herd of healthy cattle that he'd wintered with in an upper pasture. But Boss knows times are changin'. We won't be able to just let 'em roam free like we've done, sharing land with all our neighbors. He's been studying and learnin' all he can. He knows, instead of letting the cattle roam free to graze, that we have to find a way to raise enough hay to feed the cattle over each winter. And that we can't have our neighbors' cattle eatin' our feed. So we have to build fences."

She looked at the largely unspoiled valley and frowned at the thought of fences marring the beautiful undisturbed landscape. "It sounds as though everything has to change."

Dalton nodded. "It does, Lottie. Boss is a good horseman, and he'd be able to live off the sale of his horses, if he'd be willin' to sell any of 'em. But the cattle ranch is his family's heritage, and he doesn't want to fail. He'll find a way."

She smiled at Dalton, stretching her arm out until her fingers reached his for a quick caress. "He won't fail because he has men like you supporting him."

Dalton's blue eyes gleamed with the promise of joy at her soft praise. "Ah, Lottie, thank you," he whispered. They rode in silence for many minutes. He led her around a knoll and beamed as she gasped with delight. All around them, yellow flowers sprouted up in clusters, nodding in the sun.

"Are they sunflowers?" Her gaze shone with awe.

"Sort of. I guess you'd call them Montana's version of a sunflower. I'm not sure what they're called, but I've heard the native people used them for medicine and ate the roots." He hopped down and helped her dismount, so she could wander among the flowers. Taking both horses by their reins, he tied them up at a nearby bush. He held his hand out to her, breathing a sigh of relief as she clasped his.

She paused when they stood a short distance from the horses, her eyes filled with wonder. "Thank you for bringing me here. For wanting to share this with me." She ducked her chin, suddenly shy. "For arranging Davina's help today."

He ran a soft hand down her arm. "She understands my desire to spend a little time with you before we wed." He waved an arm out to the field around them. "These wouldn't be here for me to show you in a few weeks." He smiled tenderly. "If there's one thing I've learned, it's to grab at these moments of joy, for we're never promised they'll be here tomorrow."

She sobered as she met his earnest gaze. "What happens when there is a tomorrow and a tomorrow after that one? Will you be disappointed that you are saddled with me?"

Dalton shook his head once, before swooping down to kiss her. He pulled her close, wrapping his strong arms around her waist and back, digging his fingers in her hair and dislodging her hat. Everything but their embrace faded from his consciousness. No birdsong, no gentle breeze, no horse neighing in the distance interrupted his deep pleasure of cradling her in his arms again.

Releasing her, he backed away, his gaze fervent as he stared at her. "No, Lottie," he gasped, his hands caressing her shoulders. "Never. It'd mean my every prayer had been answered. To have a future ..." He paused, swallowing back words.

She stepped forward, breaching the small space between them. "I understand you're leery after the death of Mary." She said his first wife's name in a reverent tone. "What more aren't you telling me?" She stilled when she saw a flash of pain in his gaze. "What more should I know?"

He backed away, reaching for her hand. "Come. Let's gather our items for lunch." He ignored her irritated huff of breath as she walked beside him. He matched her cautious steps, walking at a slow pace to the horses. After extracting a blanket, sandwiches, and a canteen of water, he urged her again. "Come." Then he led her to a small area of shade.

He spread out the blanket, settling the food down before resting near her. With a long sigh, he finally spoke. "I'm sorry, Lottie. I know you have questions about me, just as I do about you. We'll be discovering truths about each other for as long as we're together." He stared at her panic-filled gaze. "Which I hope will be the rest of our lives." He smiled as her breath *whoosh*ed out in relief.

Dalton sat, munching on a sandwich, watching her nibble at hers. She picked at the crust, taking tiny bites. "It's fine to have an appetite," he said with a wry smile. "I won't think less of you because you don't eat like a sparrow." He smiled when she flushed. After finishing his first sandwich, he leaned back on his elbows, kicking his legs out to rest on the grass in front of them. "What would you know, Lottie?"

Her eyes rounded, as she nearly choked on a larger bite of sandwich. After taking a hasty swallow of water, she set her sandwich on the fabric of her dress. She sat with her legs crossed, and fine wisps of hair escaped from her braid down her back, making her appear much younger than twenty-seven. "Why do you avoid talking about your past?"

He sighed. "Much the same as you, I expect. If somethin' brings you pain, you avoid discussin' it." He shrugged as he chewed on a piece of grass. "Or I reckon that's what most folks do." He paused. "I was born in Ohio. We were poor, but we never felt it. Ma and Pa worked hard, and we always had food, although not always enough." He tugged out another piece of grass and twirled it in his fingers. "When the War came, I was too young to go fight. I was only eleven. I thought I'd burst with pride as I watched Pa ride off to join the battle."

Dalton paused again, his gaze distant, as though envisioning that long-ago scene. "We waited every day for word of him." He shook his head. "Never thought we'd never hear anythin'."

His voice had gone flat, as had his gaze. "Ma couldn't keep up the farm without Pa, and soon we were forced off our land. Life isn't kind to those who are poor." His gaze met hers, and he saw understanding and empathy in hers. "Too soon we were living in a shack, with Ma taking in mending and other menial tasks to try to earn money. But we were all poor in our town. Wasn't much to do."

Charlotte reached out, her hand stroking his knee. "What did you do?"

He stared dully ahead. "I was fourteen by then. Said I'd go to the big town, four hours walk away. Find some work and come get Ma and my sisters." He stared again into the distance, his gaze unfocused.

"What happened?" she whispered, her hold on his leg tightening, instinctively understanding tragedy had struck his family.

"I returned to find they had been enticed into working in a place similar to the Boudoir." He saw her eyes widen with shock. "My mother wouldn't acknowledge she knew me when I tried to force her to leave." He rubbed at a spot on his head. "Got my head bashed in and had to squander the little money I'd earned on the doctor so he'd patch me up."

"And your sisters?" she whispered.

"They were in another establishment." His voice was low. "Mortified to have me find them there but unwillin' to leave. They knew that I couldn't support all of us and that they'd soon have to return. And that, when they did, they'd be treated even worse for having the temerity to leave."

"Oh, Dalton," she breathed, crawling forward. She traced her hands down his chest before leaning forward to rest against him. When he didn't push her away, she wrapped an arm around his waist.

91

He fell backward, pulling her with him and earning a startled shriek. "Come, Lottie. You're fine. Let me hold you." He relaxed when she nestled her head against his neck, kissing the tender skin there. "There's no need to worry about me."

"Of course there is," she said around a sniffle. "You lost your family at such an early age." Pressing up, she gazed at him with wonder. "Rather than be bitter and angry, you're a good man."

"How could I be otherwise, love?" he asked, his voice roughened, as though fighting tears. "I loved my ma. My sisters. I couldn't dishonor them by dishonoring other women."

A tear leaked out, and she gazed at him with remorse. "Oh, I wish what Miss Sorcha said had been true." At his quizzical expression, she flushed. "That you'd gone to the far homestead last summer. Perhaps everything would have been different."

He smiled tenderly at her, bending an arm to rest his head on that elbow. "From where I'm at, my Lottie, things have turned out well." His expression clouded for a moment. "I hate what you suffered. I resent you knowing a moment of fear. But I can't be sad about holding you in my arms right now."

She nodded but refused to allow his attempt at levity to sway her from the serious conversation. "It's why you were so protective of me from the moment I returned." She raised a hand to cup his cheek, flushing when he turned his head to kiss her fingers.

"Yes," he murmured. "All I could think of was my sisters and what happened to them. I didn't know your story, but I knew you'd been hurt. I suspected you'd been taken advantage of. It's too common a story." He ducked his head. "I needed to find a way to make amends."

"Amends?" she gasped. She pushed up, her elbows digging into his belly. Ignoring his protestations, she scrambled away from him. "That's what you see when you look at me? A charity? A … a … pathetic woman who couldn't manage to care for herself?" She edged away from him after he rose, batting at his hands to keep him from grabbing her. "No!"

"Lottie," he whispered, his voice low and soothing. "You know that's not how it is. How it was." He stilled his movements, his hands fisted at his sides. "Dammit, I don't know how to explain. What to say."

She lifted her chin, her shoulders back, ignoring the tears dripping off her chin. "Tell me how it was. Make me understand."

"Do you know what it is to live with regret every day of your life?" he asked in a low voice, the words raspy, as though ripped from his soul. "Do you know what it is to wonder, every day, what you could have done differently? If you could have been a better son? A better man? Anything to protect and to care for those you love?"

He ran a hand through his brown hair, sending a few strands sticking up on end. "I did. Every day from the moment I rode away from them, I worried about Ma and my sisters—although I know they're probably dead by now from some horrible disease. But the not knowing is another form of agony."

He paused, his jaw clenched, as he let go of that anger with a few deep breaths. "I knew peace, Lottie, during the years I had with Mary. Something about a woman who's got a good soul can calm the doubt. Ease the never-ending ache."

Dalton looked at her with a fiery passion. "When I saw you, sobbing on your knees in the barn in February, I wanted to kill whoever dared hurt you. When I knew you'd lost your child, I wished I had the right to offer you comfort. When you defied Boss and insisted on earning your keep by cookin' for the men, I couldn't allow another to offer you the sense of security I wanted you to find only with me."

"Why?" she whispered. "I'm not like your Mary. I'm not good and pure and worthy."

He shook his head, taking a few hesitant steps in her direction, noting she didn't back away from him. "Don't you see that you are?" he whispered. "You are a decent, kind woman, who fell for the lies spouted by an evil man. You're strong and beautiful." He swallowed as his hand shook when he raised it to stroke her cheek. "I wish I knew more about you before you came to the ranch."

She gazed at him with panic and fear. "Will you wait until we speak with Warren? If you still want to marry me, after he answers your questions, I'll tell you whatever you want to know."

Dalton studied her a long moment, his thumb tracing the silky curve of her cheek. "Someday you'll have faith, Lottie. Faith that nothing you do will cause me to leave. That nothing you have done would make me lose my esteem for you." He kissed her softly, fleetingly, on her lips. "Someday."

Releasing her, he backed away a step and sat again on the blanket. "Come, love. Rest against me, as we enjoy our time away from the ranch."

Charlotte stared at Dalton, as he rested on his back, waiting patiently for her to join him. After a moment of indecisiveness, she dropped to her knees and scooted closer to lay her head on his shoulder. When his fingers played in her hair and trailed down her shoulder to her arm and back up again, she felt a deep tension ease inside her. She was unaccustomed to a man meaning what he said.

Tentatively she wrapped her arm around his waist,

resting more heavily against him. Snuggling down, she pressed one ear against his firm chest, listening to the steady beat of his heart. The gentle cadence lulled her, and she soon found herself on the verge of sleep. Never had she felt so untroubled. So safe.

"Is this all right?" she whispered.

"No," he murmured. When she stiffened and acted as though she would roll away from him, Dalton tightened his arm around her. "This is heaven. Holding you in my arms. You wanting to be here."

"I should feel guilty," she mumbled, relaxing fully against him.

"Why?" he whispered, kissing her head.

"Another is doing my job, and I'm just lying about," she said with a deep, contented sigh. Her eyelids felt heavy, and she fought falling asleep.

"Think of it as one of Davina's wedding gifts to you, darlin'." He kissed her head again. "And try not to feel guilty when she and the others continue to do nice things for you. It's just their way."

She fidgeted, her fingers playing with a thread on his shirt. "I worry I can't repay her for her kindness."

He chuckled. "None of them want repayment. Except for you to be happy."

"I am," she murmured in a sleepy voice. "Happier than I ever thought I'd be again." She tumbled into sleep, as the birds serenaded her, and Dalton's steady heartbeat reassured her all was well in her world.

CHAPTER 8

Charlotte sat beside Dalton on the ride to town in the back of one of the wagons. The early June weather was beautiful, although the deeper green of May was already fading. Too soon the land would be baked a dull brown from the unremitting summer heat. Charlotte focused on the distant mountains, trying to still her roiling nerves, as each stride by the horses took her one step closer to the woman who wanted her dead. Although she sat with her hands clenched together on her lap, she desperately needed Dalton's steadfast support. His affection.

She released her clenched hands, moving the one closest to Dalton so that it would brush against his. When he jerked at her soft contact with him, she flushed and yanked her hand away. "I beg your pardon."

"No, Lottie," Dalton said, reaching out to grip her hand. "Here," he said, lacing their hands together. When he felt the tension in her, he released her hand, slinging an arm over her shoulder to pull her closely to him. "I'm sorry we are in the back of the wagon and not riding on the front seat. Or on horseback."

"No," she gasped. "I didn't want to make a scene with my entrance into town. I prefer to arrive unnoticed, if possible."

He chuckled, the sound echoing in the ear pressed against his chest. "Ah, love, someday you'll realize you are a woman meant to be noticed. You are a woman who will always stand out." He kissed her head. "Because of your remarkable beauty and because of your indomitable spirit." When she said nothing, he spoke in a low voice, meant only for her. "Never doubt that I admire the tremendous courage it has taken for you to venture into town with us today."

She pressed into his side, her arm wrapping around his waist. Holding him like this, being embraced in this manner, had quickly become her favorite way of feeling cherished. She recalled the afternoon they had played hooky, waking from a deep slumber in his arms. Rather than ridicule her, as she had feared, he had kissed her head, and coaxed her into finding shapes in the clouds, as he regaled her with tales about Slims, Shorty, and Dixon. Laughter, peace, and a growing sense of connection were her overarching memories from that day.

"Never forget. You are not alone. You are not the woman who had to face them without support last winter, Lottie. You have all of us now." He made circles on her back. "I fear you don't fully understand what that means, as you've never experienced the full force of a MacKinnon gathering. But you will today."

"They have no reason to accept me," she murmured, her hold on him tightening. "I am nothing to them."

He made a soothing sound, his breath on the soft skin of her nape provoking a shiver. "No, darlin', that's where you are wrong. Sorcha cares about you, and, because of that, they will too."

She pushed back to stare at him, confounded by his words. "It can't be that simple."

Smiling tenderly, he nodded. "For them, it is."

Charlotte peeked over the edge of the wagon, noting they were on the edge of town. They had passed a sawmill a few moments ago, and the church was just coming into view. "We're almost there." She saw Shorty and Dixon, who were riding on horseback, move closer to the wagon, as though flanking them and protecting her.

After passing a church and a school, the wagon came to a halt at the livery across the street. Dalton eased her from his arms and vaulted out to help her down. She stood back as two men emerged from the livery, smiles bursting forth at their arrival.

"Finally ye're here," Alistair MacKinnon proclaimed, opening his arms wide to pull Sorcha in for a hug. He kissed little Harold's head, before embracing Davina and stroking a finger over Mairi's cheek. "We thought ye were comin' tomorrow."

"Nae," Sorcha said. "We ken there's plenty of work to do afore the dance, an' we wanted to help." She leaned into her eldest brother, Cailean's, embrace, whispering something in his ear. Whatever she said had him glance intensely in Charlotte's direction.

After extricating himself from Sorcha's hold, Cailean approached Charlotte. "Miss," he said with a deferential nod. His astute gaze took in Dalton's possessive hold. "I fear I've yet to make your formal acquaintance, although I do recall seeing you at the Harvest Dance."

Charlotte flushed. "Hello, sir. I am Charlotte Ingram."

"My fiancée," Dalton said with a note of challenge in his voice.

"Truly?" Cailean asked with a shocked smile. "Oh, congratulations to you both!" He shook hands with Dalton, before awkwardly patting Charlotte on her arm. "I hope you'll be very happy. When's the wedding?"

Sorcha approached and slipped her hand through Cailean's arm. "This weekend, if the pastor is amenable. 'Twould be better to no' spark any more controversy about the latest MacKinnon associate to marry."

Cailean nodded. "Aye." He smiled at Charlotte. "Welcome, Miss Ingram. I know Belle will be happy you're here, and we have a room upstairs for you." He looked at Dalton. "We'll find someplace for you."

"I'm used to sleeping in the hayloft when we come to town."

Shaking his head, Cailean turned to greet the others, leaving Charlotte and Dalton alone. "Hayloft?" Charlotte whispered. "Is that comfortable?"

He winked at her. "If you were in my arms, it would be more comfortable." He urged her forward to follow the group to the side door of the nearby house, stilling any further questions for the moment.

Warren looked up from his papers, his gaze filled with concern, although he smiled in greeting. "Dalton. Miss Ingram. Always a pleasure to see you." His office was a short distance from the livery, with the jail and the sheriff's office next door. Across the street was Annabelle's bakery, while a little farther down the boardwalk was Jessamine's print shop and the bank. Warren liked being in the center of town for both professional and personal reasons.

Originally from Philadelphia, Warren had made Bear Grass Springs home in 1881. Although he was an honorary member of the MacKinnon family, he would never be confused for a Montana cowboy, as a polished, urbane air clung to him, even though he no longer followed the most recent fashions. However, he made frequent trips to the barber to avoid the local custom of wearing his hair long. His mustache was always neatly trimmed. And he never succeeded in hiding the innate curiosity in his piercing blue eyes. Today those eyes were clouded with worry.

Dalton studied the lawyer. Although Warren was as put together as usual with a fine suit, waistcoat, and tie, he had an air of unease about him. "Lawyer," Dalton said with a nod of his head. He took off his hat and hung it on a peg by the door. "We have a matter we need discussin' with you, and we thought it better here than with too much of the family around." He paused as he saw Warren become even more leery. "In case there were things you didn't want everyone to know."

Warren nodded. "Please, sit." He motioned to the two chairs in front of his desk, as he settled into his comfortable swivel chair behind his desk. "Coffee?" he asked, as he motioned to a small stove in a corner behind them. At the shakes of their heads, Warren laced his fingers together over the pile of papers in front of him and gave his most impersonal smile. "What brings you in today?"

Charlotte cast a quick glance at Dalton before taking a deep breath. "Mr. Dalton and I are to marry." She smiled at the flash of delight in the lawyer's gaze. "However, he won't marry me unless he understands why you sent me to the ranch in February."

Warren sat back, the only sound in the room the creaking of his chair as he moved. "I see." He remained quiet as he studied Charlotte's intended.

"Do you?" Dalton asked. "If you do, you'll understand my need to know everything, so I'm able to protect my wife. My family."

Warren nodded. "An admirable desire. Although to understand everything might take days." He sighed and shook his head, raising his left hand to massage his temple as he closed his eyes. He appeared deep in thought for long minutes. Finally he said in a whisper-soft voice, "Thank you for your patience and for not peppering me with questions."

Warren looked at the couple across from him, his sharp gaze taking in the fact Charlotte had leaned closer to Dalton, and they now held hands. "I can't answer your questions now." He held up his hand as Dalton began to argue with him. "I will answer them. I promise. But the family deserves to know too. I enlisted Frederick's aid, and I could have endangered a MacKinnon." He sighed. "After all they've done for me ..." He shook his head in regret. "Tonight, at Cailean's. I promise."

Warren watched Charlotte soothe Dalton's instinctual impatience and need to know more, so that he could safeguard her from any harm. For a moment, Warren felt his spirit lighten at the man she had found for herself. A man far superior than any she had encountered in Warren's family.

Charlotte sat in the MacKinnon living room, bursting at the seams with occupants. She recognized many from the recent family dinner, although a few had arrived after dinner. All were treated like family, although she knew it was impossible that all were related, as there were only four MacKinnon siblings and one cousin, while gathered here were at least seven or eight couples and their respective children.

For some reason, two of the older children, Mildred and Hortence, had clung to Charlotte like a burr, and she now sat with one by her side and the other in front of her. She idly braided Mildred's silky black hair, while Hortence bristled with impatience for her turn. Mildred, also known as Bright Fawn, was Fidelia and Bears's eldest daughter, while Hortence was Leticia and Alistair's eldest. They were cousins and best friends.

"Unless you object to braiding hair my color," Hortence said in a low voice.

"Why should I?" Charlotte asked, as she tied off Mildred's braid, tapping her on the shoulder so the girls could trade places. She ran her hands through Hortence's beautiful red hair. "Can I let you in on a little secret?"

When Hortence stared at her wide-eyed, Charlotte lowered her voice, so the younger girl felt like the conversation was just for her—although any of the adults could still listen in, if they wanted to. "I've always wished my hair was more red than blond." She ran a hand over her hair. "Mine's always seemed a bit dull to me."

Hortence stared at her in wonder. "No, Miss Ingram, it's beautiful. I wish mine weren't so bright. It's all anyone notices about me."

Charlotte smiled softly at the girl who would soon be a young woman. "If they have no sense, that's all they'll notice. For those who are discerning, they'll look below the surface." She gasped with surprise as Hortence hopped up and hugged her.

"I'm so happy you're joining our family," she proclaimed, as Mildred nodded her agreement. "We always need more aunts."

Charlotte shook her head, stuttering, "I'm not really a member of the family."

Leticia—Hortence's mother and Alistair MacKinnon's wife—sat on a nearby chair. "If we claim you, you're family." She shrugged as though it were truly that simple.

Ducking her head as she battled a deep emotion, Charlotte watched Warren enter the room with Dalton on his heels. By this time, the MacKinnon women had effectively hemmed in Charlotte on all sides, and no space was left for

Dalton near her. She saw his frustration, as he wished to be closer to her, and she sent him an apologetic smile.

Taking a deep breath, she began to braid Hortence's hair, as she waited for Warren to speak. She feared her acceptance into the MacKinnon clan would be the shortest on record, and she'd be the latest townsperson to suffer Jessamine MacKinnon's biting wit, as she wrote about Charlotte in her newspaper.

She misbraided Hortence's hair, whispering her apology that she had to start all over again. Hortence shrugged, as Leticia laughed. "My daughter loves to have her hair played with, and I don't have the time I used to with two young children. She's delighted."

Warren cleared his throat and then clapped his hands to silence the chatter of the various groups in the room. "If I might have your attention?" He stood tall with a regal bearing, as he faced his friends, while a silence descended over the room, only broken by the babbling of infants and children. "I must impart distressing information, and I fear your anger will outweigh your goodwill toward me." His eyes gleamed with the agony of what he feared would come. "I would say, *I'm sorry*, but I know that is no excuse."

Warren cleared his throat again, interrupted from saying anything more when Cailean approached him. As the eldest MacKinnon, Cailean was the patriarch of the family, and everyone looked to him for guidance and blessings. He had found tremendous happiness in his marriage to Annabelle Evans and a delight beyond measure as a father to their daughter, Skye. "No, Warren," Cailean said, gripping his arm. "You know we might be angry with you. We might yell and blather on, as is our way. But we'd never cast you out." He looked out at the room, his gaze homing in on Charlotte. "We'll not cast out anyone present tonight." Murmurs of agreement echoed through the room at his pronouncement.

With a deep breath, Warren said, "I put Sorcha at risk. I endangered the twins." He met Frederick's intense stare. "I didn't warn you."

"Why?" Frederick asked in an irate voice. "Why. after everything?" His jaw ticked with anger.

"Shame," he said, as he closed his eyes. He jerked as his wife, Helen, snuggled up to his side, silently supporting him as she leaned into him, her arms wrapped around his waist. "I knew more than I told you in February. I intimated it was because Charlotte was my client. And she was. But it was also because I was humiliated. Again."

Sorcha gripped Frederick's arm, shaking her head. "I dinna understand, Warren. Ye've always told the truth. Ye've always been straightforward. Ye ken ye're like a brother to us all." She waited, frowning when she saw fear in Warren's gaze, rather than acknowledgment of her words. "Help us understand."

He sighed, his arms wrapping around Helen as though she were a lifeline. "My family was powerful in Philadelphia. As you know, my father was never bothered by anything so unaccommodating as scruples. I fear my mother's family was no better." He paused, gathering his thoughts. "I had cousins, although they preferred to associate with my older brother. He was going to be the successful lawyer, carrying on the family practice."

"As you recall, we remember your cousin, Jeremiah," Harold Tompkins said with a wry smile. He sat on a chair, holding his wife, Irene's, hand as he appeared completely at ease. They were Frederick's grandparents and ran the successful Sunflower Café in town.

"Jeremiah," Warren said, as he cleared his throat. "I gave up drink after his visit. And hoped I'd never see another cousin here again. That hope was unfulfilled." He looked at Charlotte a long moment. "I heard about the arrival of a man called Orville last fall. It's a common-enough name, but I feared it was my cousin. And it was."

Dalton looked from Warren to Charlotte. "Orville is the name of the man who mistreated Miss Ingram?" At Warren's nod, Dalton flushed red. "Orville Clark?"

"No, Orville Coldwell. He's from my mother's side."

"You knew your family was responsible for harming her?" Dalton asked.

Warren sighed. "Yes. He was in town last fall. We met once, a most unpleasant meeting in my office. He was upset this was such a small inconsequential town, without the promise of Butte." He ran a hand through his hair, uncaring that he set his tidy locks on end. "He was shocked that a lawyer of my talents would waste his life in such a backwater place and said my family would only ever feel shame at my lack of ambition."

Helen murmured something, easing the sting of those words.

"Only fools believe money soothes all sorrow," Bears said. He stood near Frederick and Dalton, as though prepared to hold them back if they lunged for the lawyer.

Warren nodded, cleared his throat. "While I collected my mail one morning in December, I happened to meet Charlotte, crying at the train station, as she babbled out her tale of woe, and I knew I needed to help her. I'd heard too many similar tales in the past with regard to my cousins in Philadelphia to ever doubt her story. I paid for her trip to Butte, giving her Orville's address." His gaze glowed with regret. "I sent her to hell and didn't realize it."

Dalton took a step toward him, held in place by Bears's strong hold. "Did you know he was married?"

"No," he whispered. "But when Charlotte returned here in January, bruised and battered, I knew I had to help her. For no one should have to suffer my family's wrath alone."

"*Bruised and battered*," Dalton rasped, his gaze flying to meet Charlotte's, but her gaze was downcast. Tears silently coursed down her cheeks. "Who hurt her? I thought she had tea." He struggled in Bears's hold, but the bigger man held firm.

"Yes, tea." Warren cleared his throat. "She did have tea. That was Adella's contribution to the debacle. Orville had another plan. A member of the household was entrusted with the task of ensuring she was not seen again."

Hortence and Mildred gasped, their eyes huge. Leticia rose with Fidelia, ushering the girls and the younger children from the room, as they gave Warren an exasperated glare for speaking of such topics in front of the children.

Hortence held a hand to her hair as it fell out of the braid, looking to Charlotte in dismay. Her sadness evaporated when she saw the shattered look in Charlotte's eyes. After hugging her, she followed her mama out of the room.

Dalton wrenched his arm free of Bears's hold, weaving his way through the MacKinnons to approach Charlotte, who now sat alone, as though on an island, after the departure of Leticia and the children. He sat beside her, his hand reaching out to run softly down her arm. "You're all right, Lottie. No one will hurt you here." He frowned at the MacKinnons staring at them as she remained quiet and quivering beside him, as though in shock. He looked to Warren. "What do you mean, battered and bruised? How battered? How bruised?"

Helen spoke up. "I cared for her. She was … hurt. Badly. She needed time and a safe place to recover."

Frederick waited until he heard Leticia and Fidelia chattering with the children before he faced Warren again, cutting off what more Dalton would have asked. "Warren? What do you mean when you say Sorcha and the twins were in danger?"

Closing his eyes, perhaps praying for patience or divine intervention, Warren spoke as though the words were torn from him. "My family only cares about appearances. About the prestige of the family name. My cousin wants to be the first senator when the Territory becomes a state. He's currying favor of the true Copper Kings, even as he tries to match their wealth with insignificant mines in Butte." His eyes glowed with rage as he avoided looking at Charlotte. "Something like a pregnant lover out of wedlock would only lead to embarrassment and the loss of the prestige he so desires. And would cost him an election."

"He wants me dead," Charlotte said. "As I believe Adella does too. Once I refused to give them my baby, allowing them to act as though they were the parents and the perfect political family, I was of no use to them. I worried he'd come to the ranch. Or one of his henchmen. That he'd harm one of you." Her voice broke, as she looked at Sorcha, holding Mairi, and Irene, holding little Harold.

"You are precious," Dalton rasped, his hold on Charlotte tightening. "You had every right to worry about your own safety, Lottie."

"Orville sent me an inquiry a few months ago," Warren stated, "asking if I'd heard from Charlotte. He must mistrust me, and the curt answer I sent back, for he sent Adella to investigate. I knew her from Philadelphia. She's like Orville, as ambitious and as unfettered by anything nearing a moral code. She's been here close to two weeks."

"Why not tell me?" Frederick asked. He shook his head as his grandfather attempted to soothe him with a calm word. "No. I am a father. A husband. I have men who look to me for guidance. I am their boss." His jaw twitched with barely suppressed rage. "How could you have left us open to an adversary we didn't even know about?"

Warren held up a hand and shrugged. "I'm sorry, Fred. I

... thought I'd escaped them. I never imagined the lure of riches in a hill in Montana would induce them to leave Philadelphia. And that they would then harm the family I adore."

Sorcha strode to Frederick, thrusting Mairi into her husband's arms. She understood that, if Frederick were holding his daughter, he'd be unable to fight Warren. "Ye let us down, Warren."

He flinched as though she had struck him. "I know. I betrayed you."

Holding her hands on her hips, she shook her head. "Nae, I didna say that. Ye did no' say ye betrayed me or my family in yer tale. Ye let me down. I've relied on yer friendship. On ye lookin' out for me an' those I love." She sighed as she pushed forward, wrapping her arms around him, as Helen stepped aside to allow them to have a moment together. "Who's been lookin' out for ye, ye dear man?"

"Sorcha," he gasped, holding her close a moment.

She pushed back. "It doesna mean I'm no' angry with ye. Ye should have told us what was occurrin' from the beginnin'." She spun to stare at Charlotte to include her in her pronouncement. "But I understand fear, an' I ken it doesna make ye rational." She looked at her husband. "Aye, Frederick?"

He sighed, kissing his daughter's head. "Aye, love."

Warren shook his head, a dazed look in his gaze. "Does this mean I'm still your friend?" he asked the room in general.

"Nae," Cailean said, his accent thickened, as it always was when he was affected by deep emotions. "Nae, Warren, ye're family, as ye always have been."

Warren closed his eyes, one arm wrapped around Helen again. After taking another deep breath, he looked to Frederick and then Dalton. "Charlotte would have been safer on the ranch."

"You want her to hide forever?" Dalton asked. "No, lawyer. That's not a life, and she deserves more than that."

"Well said," Harold called out. Young Hortence ran into the room, momentarily distracting Harold by whispering into his ear. Rising, he followed her to the kitchen, Irene on his heels.

Ewan, the youngest MacKinnon brother, spoke up. "Aye, that's true, but I doubt Warren's cousins are comfortable outside of what they consider civilization." He smiled. "The ranch would seem wild to them."

Warren nodded. "Yes, although they can ride horses." He shrugged self-deprecatingly. "Although never as well as a cowboy."

Ewan focused on Dalton, sitting beside Charlotte. "Why did ye truly come to town?"

Charlotte squeezed Dalton's hand. "To marry. We want the preacher's blessing."

Ewan's wife, Jessamine, smiled as though she had just been handed the keys to a bank safe. "Ah, you do know how to make a reporter happy." She beamed at them, as she held her daughter, Aileana, against her chest.

"A preacher's blessing won't bring you any more clarity," Bears said.

Charlotte frowned at his cryptic words. "I want to marry Dalton. I want …" She shrugged, as Bears continued to stare at her with a wise understanding that unnerved her. She fidgeted on the settee, only calming when Dalton whispered in her ear.

Frederick looked to Warren. "Come," he said in his authoritative manner. "Let's eat Belle's cake, and then we can determine what we should do." He shared a meaningful glance with the men in the room, before motioning everyone back into the kitchen.

Charlotte clung to Dalton a moment. "Are you mad at me?" she whispered.

"No, love, not at you," he whispered, as he kissed her cheek. "Warren's cousin better never show his face here." He rose, holding out his hand to escort her into the kitchen.

After a moment's hesitation, Charlotte placed her hand in his. She wanted to ask so much more. Wanted to say so much more. But she knew too many people loitered about, and she wanted privacy for her conversation with Dalton. She was uncertain how she'd find a quiet moment with this bustling family ever present.

That night Charlotte tossed and turned in her bed in Cailean's house. Although the bed was more comfortable than any she'd ever slept in, she could not settle. Her mind played the evening's discussion over and over again, and she resented that she hadn't had a chance to speak with Dalton alone. He had departed with the other men to talk with Warren, leaving her in silent misery with the MacKinnon women. Although they were supportive, she had needed Dalton's reassurance. Now that he knew the truth, would he marry her?

A soft tap on her door had her sitting up. "Yes?"

Annabelle poked her head inside. "Are you well? I wanted to see if you needed anything before I head to bed." She frowned as she saw the tangled bedclothes. "You're more unsettled now than when you listened to Warren speaking." Leaving the door ajar, she entered the guest room and perched on the side of the bed.

Charlotte attempted to paste on a serene expression, but her eyes revealed her torment. When Annabelle remained quiet, a knowing look in her gaze, any of Charlotte's false serenity evaporated. Her shoulders curled forward, and she hit the mattress with a fist. "I couldn't speak with him. I need to speak with him if I'm to have any chance of sleeping."

"Warren?" Annabelle asked.

"No, Dalton," Charlotte cried out in a near plaintive wail. "He seemed supportive while Warren spoke, but then he disappeared. What must he think of me?"

"I don't understand," Annabelle whispered, gripping her hand that remained fisted on the mattress. When Charlotte remained quiet, Annabelle rose. "Give me a few minutes," she murmured, as she left the room.

Charlotte sighed, flopping to her back on the bed. "I've even scared Anna away," she whispered, rolling to her side and burying her face in a pillow. She'd learned long ago how to sob without making any noise, and she let her tears flow quietly, her shaking shoulders the only sign of her distress.

A soft hand caressed her upper back, and Charlotte shifted in the bed to look over her shoulder. "Dalton," she whispered. "I never thought they'd let you in here."

"Only for a short time," Annabelle said, as she poked her head into the room. "As far as the townsfolk know, Dalton's having a drink with Cailean in the sitting room." Annabelle smiled at the distressed couple. "Call out if you need anything, Charlotte. And, Dalton, I'll send Cailean in if you're here too long. You need to spend the night in the back room at the bakery, or there will be talk."

Cailean poked his head in over his wife's and studied the couple. "We could always say he fell asleep on the sitting room floor." He grunted as Annabelle elbowed him in his side. "You'll have a better sleep here. Otherwise, if you're spending the night at the bakery, Belle shows up at daybreak to start baking." He tugged Annabelle out of the doorway, winking at them, as he murmured the decision was theirs.

"I don't understand," Charlotte whispered.

"He's giving us the choice, if we want to spend the night together or if we want to wait until our marriage." He frowned as he saw her stiffen. "I wouldn't do anything more than hold you, Lottie. I'd never compromise you. It would be like the night we spent on the ranch, when everyone was away."

She flushed and lowered her lashes. "I don't know why I continually worry. It's not as though I have a reputation to protect."

He made a grunt of disagreement. "Aye, you do. As my wife. As the mother of my children." He raised her hand to kiss it. "Don't let the past taint what we will have, love."

She rested on her side, gazing deeply into his troubled eyes. "Do you still dream of that future with me? Even after all Warren revealed?"

Dalton frowned, his hand rising to cup her cheek. "How can you doubt?" he whispered. "When I heard that you'd returned bruised and battered—" He swallowed. "Why didn't you tell me, Lottie?"

A tear tracked down her cheek. "I already felt like a feeble woman. To have you know the extent I'd been punished ..." She closed her eyes with shame.

"Not punished. Abused," he corrected. "No one should ever have believed they had the right to treat you in such a manner." He gazed deeply into her eyes. "Do you know the terror that filled me tonight?" At her soft shake of her head, he whispered, "I realized I'd already almost lost you but been unaware of it. I knew you'd suffered and had fought back after losing your babe, but I hadn't realized he'd also attempted to murder you."

She ducked her head. "Ambition is a powerful incentive."

"Not for me," he said. "Honoring you and what we have is all the incentive I need." He let out a deep breath. "I know I will do things that will scare you. That will remind you of the past."

She placed her fingers over his lips. "I don't want to think of any of that."

"I can't bear the thought of unconsciously hurting you." His eyes gleamed with sincerity.

"You won't," she reassured him.

He looked around the room, rising to pull a chair out of the corner. After setting it beside the bed, he sat and leaned forward, resting on his elbows. His hands played with hers, and he gazed into her eyes. "Trust me," he murmured. "Tell me about your past. You know I don't care what Warren said."

"How can you be certain?" she whispered.

He smiled, his thumb tracing the smoothness of one of her fingernails. "Because, if Warren had revealed you'd killed either or both of them, I would have rejoiced. I wouldn't have felt one moment of remorse, other than that it was a memory you had to live with." He paused, settling into his position, canted forward, as he studied her.

"Come. Rest beside me as I tell you about me," she murmured, scooting backward in the bed. Her eyes flared as the bed squeaked in protest with her movement.

Chuckling, Dalton kicked off his boots and crawled under the covers fully dressed. He settled beside her, holding out an arm, so she could rest her head on his shoulder. Rather than insist she begin her tale, he gifted her with silence. After many long minutes, he sighed.

"I'm not asleep," she murmured. "I never realized men like to hold a woman."

"I don't know about men, but I know I do," he said, his chest rumbling under her ear. His fingers played with her hair.

"You know what it is to be wanted," she murmured. "To have parents who wanted you."

When she fell silent, he said in a soft voice, "Yes."

"I've never been wanted." She pressed her head against his chest to avoid looking at him and seeing pity. "Not the way I've seen the women of this family wanted by their husbands. Or the children cherished by their parents."

His fingers continued their soothing pattern over her cotton-covered skin. "I don't understand."

"My first memory is falling to the ground, after receiving a slap, because I displeased my grandmother. My mother stood by and laughed." Charlotte spoke in a monotone, as though the memories she related had occurred to a distant acquaintance. "I quickly learned I had to earn affection. I would never be enough."

"What more did they do?" he asked, as he kissed the top of her head.

"I began to clean houses and to work by the time I was six or seven, and I learned to cook by the time I was nine. I preferred the kitchen because I had proof of my worth there. A well-baked cake. A delicious cookie. A well-seasoned stew."

He growled with discontentment. "You'll never cook again."

"No," she protested, pressing up to stare down at him, her hair shimmering red-gold in the faint lamplight. "I … It's what I know to do."

He paused, his panting breath heating her cheek. His determined gaze met her desperate one. "You have nothing to prove to me."

"I will until the day I die," she breathed, dropping down to rest on his chest. "I'll forever be in your debt."

"I don't want you in my debt, Lottie. I don't want you believing you have to earn my affection. My esteem. My lo

—" He broke off. "Tell me more about your childhood. Your life before you arrived at the ranch."

She shrugged. "I became a proficient cook and ran the kitchen for a small café in my town. My grandmother and mother guarded me. Never wanted me to meet a man, for fear I'd run away, and they'd lose their edge over the competing cafés." She stiffened. "One night the kitchen stove caught fire, and our café burned to the ground. We lost everything."

"Oh, Lottie, I'm so sorry." He kissed her ear.

"I was dumbfounded. How could a fire have started? I'd banked the fire. I'd done nothing different from hundreds of other nights." She burrowed farther into his embrace. "But my mother accused me of wantonly destroying our livelihood and home. And she cast me out."

Dalton murmured soft words, although she could feel a tension thrumming through him. "I recall you saying you never ate well until you came to the ranch. That makes no sense if you were a cook. You had food all around you."

"If I took one taste test too many of the food, I had my knuckles swatted. If I nibbled at a cookie that crumbled, I was denied my meager portion of dinner. If I took a sip of milk, I was denied milk in my coffee for a month."

"What?" Dalton exclaimed, rolling so she was on her side, and he looked down at her. "They denied you food when you worked in a kitchen? When you brought them riches?"

She shrugged as she fought tears. "It's how I earned my worth."

"No, love. No." He closed his eyes and pressed his forehead against hers. "You are worthy simply because you are you. You need do nothing for me to value you. I will repeat this, over and over again, until you believe it. I will show you this, over and over again, until you never doubt. Please, Lottie. They abused and took advantage of you since you were a young girl. And then they threw you out. Why? Why not just build another café?"

She flushed. "I heard my mother whisper that she hoped I'd meet a wealthy benefactor, who would provide for the entire family. Tossing me out was her way of introducing me to the world."

Dalton stared at her in befuddlement. "She threw a naive and beautiful young woman out into a merciless world and hoped you'd escape unscathed? It makes no sense."

"Mama wanted me to go to Butte. Find a wealthy miner. But I disobeyed her. I disembarked the train here. I liked the look of the town." At the proud glint in his eyes, she said in a hesitant voice, "I thought that, if they had disowned me, I had the right to determine my own future."

"And you did." After a moment, he murmured, "Why'd you take such a dislike to Slims?"

She flushed. "He terrified me. Huge beast of a man. Arrogant and thought he could order me around. I had finally realized I could bake and cook what I wanted. That I could eat a little of it too. I didn't want to have to answer to him or to anyone." She flushed. "And I hated the rumors I had heard on the ranch before we left. That Miss Sorcha had hoped she would be successful in her matchmaking with us."

"She was matchmaking?"

"That's what Dixon told Shorty."

"If he told Short, then Slims knew, and he would have been ornery," Dalton said. "I've never met a man who likes to be maneuvered."

Charlotte bit her lip before blurting out, "I'd thought I'd escaped my mama's and grandmama's control, and, to be here, on a ranch, with another woman trying to manipulate me, was almost more than I could bear." She let out a huff of breath. "I was angry. And I took it out on Slims and Shorty."

"Do you even know if it was true?"

Shrugging, Charlotte shook her head ruefully. "And then I met him. Orville. And I thought he was what a real gentleman should be. Solicitous. Kind. Nothing like the rough men I'd met on the ranch." She ducked her head in apology for including Dalton in that statement. "I knew Orville was rich, and I thought I would make Mama proud by marrying a wealthy man. Finally I'd earn her love. I'd do something right."

"Oh, Lottie," he whispered, sorrow lacing his tone.

Tears leaked out, and she whispered, "I was too naive and too gullible to realize he had no regard for me either." Sniffling, she spoke, in a barely audible voice, "No one ever has."

"That's not true, darlin'," he whispered, wrapping his arms around her. He held her as she settled against him, not pressing her for any more details about her past. The little he knew would fuel his anger and fill his nightmares for years to come.

"Hold me," she whispered, as her voice thickened with sleep. "Never let me go." She slipped into sleep in his warm embrace.

CHAPTER 9

Charlotte clung to Dalton's hand as they walked from Cailean's house to the outskirts of town. MacKinnons flanked them to the front and back, and she felt cocooned by their friendship and support. Strains of dueling fiddles grew louder as each step brought them closer to the dance, and she saw Sorcha swaying from side to side with excitement to finally be in town for the Founders' Day Dance.

A severe bout of shyness had overcome Charlotte all day after her late-night conversation with Dalton. Even though she had fallen asleep in his arms, she had woken alone, her fingers searching for his warmth and comforting embrace. Until they had departed for the dance, she had only seen him at the midday meal, where he had been occupied, talking with Warren and a few of the brothers. She had enjoyed listening to the women chatter, with no expectation that she would join the conversation. Never had she known such camaraderie. However, she had wished she sat beside Dalton. She missed his quiet companionship and the reassurance of her hand in his.

Now she focused on their short walk. From Cailean's

house, the dance was nearby, just across the main street near the whitewashed church and school. Wagons crowded the area at the outskirts of town, with families traveling in from their nearby ranches and farms. Many would sleep in their wagons, as few could afford a night in the hotel or were fortunate enough to have family in town with room to spare. Charlotte gripped Dalton's arm, thankful that she had been offered friendship from the MacKinnons and that she was not consigned to an evening sleeping under the stars. With a quick glance down Main Street, she noted that all the businesses, except for the saloons, were closed.

As they approached the dance area, she smiled at the tables laden with food, while an entire section was saved for Annabelle's and Leena's baked goods. Children stomped on the grass, an attempt to make the dance floor, although Charlotte suspected their parents were hoping they'd rid themselves of some of their pent-up energy before they got into too much trouble. A few chairs were scattered on the side of the dancing area and also near the food tables, for those who needed to sit. However, most people stood and mingled. All the single women knew they'd be sought out for dancing, as there were far more men than women.

"I never thought so many people would be here," Charlotte whispered to Dalton.

"Oh, yes. The men from the mining town always come down, and the nearby ranchers and farmers came into town too. It's why the hotel is so full." He nodded in the direction of a beanpole of a man. "Mr. Atkins relishes these days, as he can hike up his prices and can charge an arm and a leg for the meager food he serves in his hotel dining room."

"Why they'd eat there rather than in our café, I'll never understand," said a gray-haired and slightly stooped man with a hitch in his gait, as he slapped Dalton on his shoulder. "I'm Harold Tompkins—Frederick's grandpa and Jane's great-uncle. We weren't properly introduced last evenin'." He beamed at who he'd call *the young'uns*. "Mighty fine to see a beautiful woman on the arms of one of my favorite men."

"Sir," Dalton said with a tip of his hat.

"Ireney," Harold bellowed, waving over a gray-haired woman with an apron around her beautiful pink dress. "Can't get her to take off her darned apron. Everywhere she goes, she insists on helping." He kissed her cheek and then beamed at Dalton. "Our boy's taken a shine to someone again."

"Oh, Dalton," Irene said, her light-blue eyes twinkling with joy. "Finally." She pushed forward, separating Charlotte from Dalton as she enfolded him in a hug. When she released Dalton, she paused as she studied Charlotte. "I recall you."

Flushing, Charlotte stammered, "I worked on the ranch last summer. I ... You might have seen me at the Harvest Dance last fall."

"When that boor from the East was passing through," Harold said with disgust. "Little of any good comes from the East."

"Harold," Irene chided. "We're all from the East, and we're all good people."

"Aye, but we've had the good sense to be here for years." He focused on Charlotte again. "Do you plan on breaking our boy's heart? He's suffered enough already."

"Harold," Irene scolded with a shake of her head. "Really, you are incorrigible."

Dalton grinned. "He hasn't changed from the moment I met him, Miss Irene."

Charlotte stared at the older couple, a sudden intense yearning filling her for such a stalwart pair intent on ensuring her happiness. "I hope to marry him."

"Marry!" Harold hollered, his arms in the air as he gave a hoot. "Is that why you're in town?"

"Partly," Dalton said, unable to suppress a grin at the old man's antics. "I'd hoped to speak to you privately, but the café was too busy today. We told the family last night, but you had left the room to be with the children." He flushed as Irene kissed his cheek.

"'Bout time, my boy, 'bout time," Harold said, beaming, as he rocked back on his heels and held on to his suspenders. "Never can have enough weddin's and good fortune."

"Well, first we must talk with the pastor. I fear he won't want to marry us on Sunday." Dalton failed to hide his worry from them.

"Then you'll marry tomorrow," Irene said. "Saturdays are beautiful days for weddings, and we'll have another excuse for a party." She beamed at Charlotte and Dalton. "Oh, I'm so glad I lived to see this day."

Dalton sobered. "No talk of anything happenin' to you, Miss Irene."

Harold wrapped an arm around his wife's waist. "Oh, she's fine. Aren't you, darlin'?" he asked, as he kissed her head. "Just sentimental. We want all our boys settled before ... Well, before." His blue eyes gleamed. "We aren't gettin' any younger."

"Well, with any luck, you'll witness my ... our marriage tomorrow."

The lively fiddle music slowed to a waltz, and Dalton eased Charlotte onto the dance floor. In spite of the fact that he'd stood beside her for over an hour, her hand clasped in his, he knew nothing would relieve his desire to hold her in his arms. He chuckled when she shrieked as he twirled them around. "Ah, you're a delight, Lottie." He lowered his head, so it rested near hers.

She shivered at being held so closely in his arms. "You are the most fortunate of men."

He laughed, kissing her cheek. "You've finally discovered that?" he teased. "I'm holding the most beautiful woman at the dance in my arms and will marry her tomorrow. I couldn't be more fortunate."

She flushed, whispering, "Thank you," at his compliment. "No, I meant you have so many concerned for you." She arched away to stare into his inquisitive blue eyes. "You have no idea what it would mean to have one person care for me as all of these here do for you."

"But you do, Lottie," he murmured.

She flushed and broke her gaze from his. "Forgive me for being envious." When he shifted his hold on her, so one arm remained at her waist and the other cupped her cheek, she wrapped both of her arms around his neck. "I wished I had had a Harold or an Irene in my life."

"Ah, Lottie, I wish you'd had them too. But now you do," he said. "They can be overbearing—can interfere at times—but they are loving." He sighed with regret as the waltz came to an end. "Come, love. Let's join the others. It'll give you time to plot tomorrow." He bumped into a startlingly attractive black-haired woman with her voluptuous figure in a sapphire satin dress. "Beg your pardon, ma'am."

"You should be sorry, you degenerate cowpoke," she said in a low voice. "I thought it an aberration of all I hold good and true in this world when I learned that an upstanding man would deign to marry this woman." She spoke in a nasally disgusted voice, as she pointed at Charlotte.

"Ma'am, you're making a scene, and I cannot abide anyone speaking poorly about my bride," Dalton said in a soft voice, laced with warning.

"Bride?" she gasped. "So you've already married this woman and turned your life into a travesty?"

Dalton's hand gripped Charlotte's tightly. "We marry on the morrow. And, if you are so kind, we'd appreciate it if you were not present."

"I don't care what you appreciate. This woman's a harlot. She relishes attempting to steal other women's husbands. Did she tell you that?" Her brown eyes flashed with anger, as she waved at Charlotte, standing slightly behind Dalton. "Look at how she cowers behind you. She can't even admit to her own maliciousness."

"My malicious deeds?" Charlotte rasped. "You ... witch."

"I take it you are related to Warren Clark?" Dalton asked. He looked up to see that the MacKinnons had wended their way around them, forming a buffer between them and the townsfolk. Only if the woman yelled would anyone in town be the wiser to what she proclaimed.

"I am Adella Coldwell. I am here to right a wrong and to prevent another man from being duped by this deceiver." Adella stood as tall as her short frame allowed, her hands on her shapely hips. She posed as though she understood the power the feminine form had on addling men's reason.

"Adella, such a shame to see you again," Warren murmured in his cultured voice. "I'm certain you are deliriously anxious to make the acquaintance of my wife, Helen." He motioned for her to follow him, frowning when she stayed rooted in place.

Adella forced a smile, as she stared at her husband's cousin. "Warren, always a pleasure. I can't believe it's been so long since I saw you at the cultured soirees in Philadelphia."

"Yes, in the true viper's den," he murmured. "Tell me. I'm curious to understand. How did you come to learn that my good friend, Dalton, was to marry before he did?"

Adella faltered for only a moment. "Of course that is what he'd claim. I have it on good authority that this entire charade was planned. From the moment she"—Adella waved in Charlotte's direction, ignoring her ashen countenance —"wrote, informing me of her plan to find a man to ensnare."

"Lies," Charlotte whispered. "I never wrote you." When Warren glared her into silence, she bit her lip, silencing any protestation of her innocence.

"I presume you'd travel with such incriminating evidence. Surely you'd understand that one such as I would demand to see the proof of what you claim," Warren said. He smiled ferally as Adella paled. "Your tricks worked in Philadelphia because those in the drawing rooms cared what you said. They relished in destroying young women's futures because it brought them entertainment in a world devoid of purpose." He shook his head. "We have purpose here. And little patience for intrigue or lies."

"What man wants to marry a woman who's shown such poor judgment that she throws away her virtue on a married man?" Adella smiled as she saw Charlotte flinch at that comment. "I'd think she would reconsider her choice in him. He'll only see her as a drudge and second best. She'll wonder, forever, if he is perpetually disappointed that he didn't wait for someone better."

"You spiteful bi—" Dalton broke off what he would have said when he looked at Charlotte's devastated gaze. "I've had enough. You have no right to speak such malicious lies. You have no right to hurt Miss Ingram." He wrapped an arm around Charlotte and moved into the tight circle of MacKinnons and friends awaiting them. Looking over his shoulder, he saw Warren speaking in an intense low voice to the interloper. "Lottie," Dalton murmured to her.

"*Shh*," she murmured. "Just hold me. Please."

He enfolded her in his arms, wishing he were a poet and had the words to soothe the pain Adella provoked.

"That woman's nothin' but trouble," Harold murmured to

Dalton, his gaze flitting from Warren to Dalton. He nodded with approval to see Dalton soothing a trembling Charlotte. "I hope you have sense and keep your intended away from her."

A few hours later the long Montana evening was finally turning toward twilight, and the dance was on the verge of breaking up. However, Harold marched up to the small stage area, where the fiddlers played, and whistled to gain everyone's attention. "I know you'll think I'm impertinent, but by now you know that's my nature." He laughed as the townsfolk heckled him. "I have a surprise for you, and now seems the appropriate time, as the evening cools and we're all stuffed to the gills after the delicious food."

"Get on with it, old man!" Irene called out.

He puffed out his chest, hooking his hands through his suspenders, as he tilted his head up. "I would, Ireney, if you'd let me." He chuckled along with the townsfolk. "Now you might not be aware, but, in my family, we have two of the best singers in the Territory. I've convinced them to serenade us, and, if we're lucky, they'll sing more than one song."

The townsfolk murmured as Sorcha and Davina approached the stage. Sorcha whispered something to the fiddlers and then nodded. Linking hands, the two cousins closed their eyes and sang in an unknown language. Their voices were pure, harmonious, and called to Charlotte's soul. Although she had no idea what they were saying, she sensed a deep longing, a mourning in the song, and tears welled in her eyes.

Someone nudged her shoulder, and she looked up and up into the teasing eyes of Slims. "I know you think they're singing of a lost homeland or losing someone they love.

They're probably talking about a passionate encounter with a fairy. We'll never be the wiser."

She giggled and shook her head, as he winked at her and moved away to speak with Frederick. Dalton remained with her, holding her close, as he rested his chin atop her head, swaying them softly side to side.

When the first song ended, the townsfolk roared, and Sorcha and Davina agreed to sing one more. Equally transfixed during the second song, Charlotte sighed, as Dalton kissed her cheek.

At the eruption of applause, she fought clinging to him as he eased away. "I must speak with the preacher," he murmured.

"I want to congratulate Sorcha and Davina." She ran a hand down his arm. "I'll meet you here in a few moments."

"Good, for I'm certain the man will want to ensure you desire to wed me tomorrow." He stared deeply into her gaze, unable to hide the uncertainty in his. When she cupped his cheek and nodded, he smiled fully. "Good."

Charlotte turned to speak with Sorcha and Davina, only to find her way marred by a mob of townsfolk. As she waited on the edge of the large group, Adella sidled up to her. "I have nothing to say to you."

"That's fine because I have plenty to say to you," Adella said. She leaned forward. "How dare you believe you can start over again after what you did?"

"I did nothing but believe the lies of a worthless man," Charlotte said, taking pride that her voice only wavered a little. She hoped that weakness was concealed by the boisterous crowd noise.

"You had the opportunity to give me what I most desired. And you denied me!" Adella shook her head, as though that were inconceivable. "How could you?"

Charlotte faced her, her cheeks a mottled red. "How could you have treated me as you did? Serving me that tea?"

Staring at her in confusion, Adella said, "I always serve my guests tea. Why wouldn't I you?" She waved away Charlotte's complaint. "Your selfishness brought about your pain."

"My selfishness?" Charlotte gasped. "It was my baby. Never yours."

Adella's eyes gleamed with a deep agony. "Yes, I know." She closed her eyes. "You proved that I am truly the barren one in my marriage. Not my husband. Do you know what that does to a woman?" she asked, turning away.

"It doesn't give you the right to do what you did," Charlotte snapped.

"Asking you to give us your child was wholly appropriate." She closed her eyes. "Coming here to beg you to reconsider was foolish." She stared at Charlotte with loathing. "I can see you found a way to rid yourself of your bothersome problem. It took you no time to find another willing man. Did he rebel against the idea of raising another man's bastard?"

Charlotte stared at her in horror. "How can you deny what you did?"

"How can you deny what you are?" Adella said with scorn in her gaze. "You lie and cheat and then try to blame another for what you've done. You think I'm vile, when you should focus on yourself." She paused, taking a deep breath, and spat out spitefully, "You seem to have no trouble cozying up to another man so soon after you claim to have loved my husband. Are you so fickle that one man is as good as another?" She traced a finger down Charlotte's arm in a mockery of the caresses Dalton had gifted her.

"Or are you so desperate for any man's attention that you'll accept anyone's touch?" Adella smiled as Charlotte gasped in agony at her words. "Is that how you feel when he holds you in bed too? Do you compare his touch to my husband's and long for the refined touch of a man who knows how to treat a woman?" She lowered her voice. "Or perhaps you're stupid enough to believe your cowboy's lies, when he tells you that you are special and unique and lovely."

Charlotte jerked away. "I've heard enough." She stumbled until she was alone at the side of the party that was beginning to break up, her mind spinning.

Dalton approached the new pastor, feeling a trickle of sweat down his spine. He suddenly wished he'd accepted a swig from Ewan's flask, although he knew it would have done little to help him through this interview. When the couple conversing with the new pastor and his wife departed, Dalton approached, swiping at his hair and wishing he were more polished.

"Sir. Pastor. Mr. Fitch," he stammered, shifting from foot to foot as his words dried up.

The man, who appeared about Dalton's age, stared at him with a benevolent smile, enhancing his rather plain features into those of an engaging and handsome man. "I'm Pastor Fitch, and it's a pleasure to meet you."

"Sir," Dalton stammered. "Ma'am. It's lovely to meet you, Mrs. Fitch." He nodded to the slightly younger woman standing beside the pastor with hair that shone like the color of rich pecans. He paused, momentarily awestruck by the wondrous beauty of her eyes. Neither green nor gray, they seemed a mixture of the two. When she laughed, he flinched.

"I'm Miss Fitch, kind sir," she said. "Pastor Fitch's sister."

"Oh," Dalton said. "It's nice to make your acquaintance." He nodded again, before taking a deep breath. "You don't know me, Pastor, but I hoped you'd be willin' to marry me tomorrow. My fiancée and I are here in town, and we'd like a proper wedding."

Studying Dalton, he sobered. "And you feared I'd decline," he said in a deep, melodious voice. His brown hair blew in the breeze, and his brown eyes looked troubled as he shook his head.

"Please, Pastor," Dalton entreated. "We don't know when we'll be back again, and we want a proper weddin'. I want no one to doubt the validity of our union."

Pastor Fitch nodded. "I wasn't denying that I'd perform the ceremony tomorrow, young man, for I don't know your name. I'm upset you'd ever doubt I'd perform it. I fear the man who presided over the congregation before me had a different attitude over what was reasonable."

"I'm Dalton, sir. I work on Frederick Tompkins's ranch. The Mountain Bluebird." He cast a glance over his shoulder. "I can't see her right now due to the crowd, but I'm to marry Miss Ingram. She's our cook." His eyes glowed with pleasure at the thought.

Grinning, Pastor Fitch looked at his sister. "Well, it seems he's delighted. Let's find the bride to determine if she's as eager." He held out his arm, and his sister walked beside him, as they wended their way through the crowd that had begun to disperse.

Dalton approached Frederick, who stood with Sorcha by his side. She flushed and nodded as townsfolk continued to applaud her talent. Dalton noted Davina standing beside Slims. "Miss Sorcha, have you seen Charlotte?"

Sorcha shook her head. "No, but 'tis a bit chaotic." She focused on the man beside Dalton. "Are ye the new preacher?" She gazed at him assessingly, when he nodded. "I hope ye are more discernin' in who ye favor an' who ye ridicule while standin' in yer pulpit each Sunday."

Frederick whispered, "Hush," in her ear, introducing

himself and Sorcha to the man and his sister. "We're delighted to meet you."

"Aye," Sorcha said, ignoring her husband's warning. "But ye must ken my husband an' his family have suffered enough pain from the lashings they've already received from the pulpit."

Pastor Fitch shifted uncomfortably. "I'm a different sort of pastor. I know only time will prove that to be true."

"Come," Dalton said, as he spotted Charlotte. "She's over there."

"Be sure to come to the party tomorrow, Pastor!" Sorcha called.

"Party?" Miss Fitch asked. "Didn't we just have one tonight?"

Dalton flushed, and his smile was embarrassed but grateful. "They are throwing another one tomorrow after our weddin'. If you refused, Warren, the lawyer, would have married us." He approached Charlotte, becoming more grave as she had lost some of her innate vitality. "Lottie?" he whispered. "I've found the pastor."

She mustered a smile and reached for his hand before snatching hers back again. She gazed at him with a confused, tormented expression. "I don't know what to do."

He settled his hands on her shoulder, lowering his head closer to her. His musky scent with a hint of sandalwood cologne and horses wafted over her, and it was as though the two of them were alone in a sea of people. "Lottie, what happened?"

"I fear I've been a fool," she whispered. "That what I thought was true was a lie."

He paled. "Do you want me to ask the preacher to leave?"

Her hand instinctively reached for him, and she shook her head. "No. No. I want to marry you, Dalton. But there's so much I don't understand. So much ..." She sighed as he eased her into his arms. After standing stiffly for a moment, she relaxed, melting into his supportive embrace.

"Will you tell him that?" he whispered, his soft breath warming her neck. "You must reassure him that I'm not forcing you."

"Forcing me?" she asked, backing up to shake her head and to stare at him as though he were acting like a ninny. "Of course you aren't." She craned her neck to look over Dalton's shoulder at the pastor, waiting patiently behind her betrothed. "Of course he isn't. I want to marry him."

She saw the kind, rather plain man smile with relief. Wriggling, she eased from Dalton's arms. "I am Charlotte Ingram. I am eager to marry Dalton tomorrow."

"Miss Ingram, I am Pastor Fitch. This is my sister, Miss Fitch."

Charlotte smiled at both of them. "It's lovely to meet you."

Dalton held her close by his side, talking with the pastor about the time for the wedding the following day, before leading them back to introduce him and his sister to the ranch hands. The pastor had met the MacKinnons but only in a remote way. As he watched the pastor and his sister interact with the engaging group, he was unable to stop thinking about the change in Charlotte's demeanor toward him. What had occurred? Why was she acting so differently? More important, how could he reassure her that everything would be fine and that nothing needed to change between them?

CHAPTER 10

Dalton stood at the front of the church near the altar, waiting for Charlotte to walk down the aisle toward him. He attempted to paste on a confident expression, but he feared Slims could see through him. He turned away from the friends and the townsfolk who had gathered to witness his union with Charlotte, resolutely ignoring Dixon's amusement at his distress.

"Ignore him," Slims murmured to Dalton. "Dix will have his day, and then you can remind him what an idiot he was to you."

Dalton let out a shaky breath. "Were you this nervous?" he whispered.

Shrugging, Slims nodded. "But I'll never admit to it if you tell anyone." He smiled in a self-deprecating manner. "Are you afraid she won't show up or because you doubt your decision?"

Dalton speared his friend with a tormented glance. "I'm afraid she regrets her decision. And I couldn't live with myself if I'm binding myself to a woman who will always resent me."

Slims stared at him with a perplexed expression. "What I'd remember is that she had no doubts, until she saw that woman last night. Perhaps something happened." He snapped his jaw shut and looked over his shoulder as the congregation hushed.

As their wedding gift to Charlotte, Sorcha and Davina had agreed to sing again, as Charlotte walked down the aisle. The duo sang an uplifting, hopeful-sounding song as first Sorcha and then Davina walked down the aisle, holding small bouquets of the wild yellow flowers that had entranced Charlotte last week.

Dalton faced the procession, his breath catching as Charlotte slipped her arm through Warren's. Her light-blue silk dress enhanced her natural beauty, and her hair shone in the church window's sunlight. She carried a larger bouquet of the wild yellow flowers.

"Bears heard her story about how much she loved the flowers, and he walked to a mountaintop to find them for her," Slims murmured.

Dalton made a noise, meant to acknowledge what Slims said, his whole focus on Charlotte. He gazed deeply into her beautiful sherry-colored eyes, hoping his gaze conveyed his steadfastness. His loyalty. His heart stuttered. *His love.* Searching her gaze for any sign she felt the same, he battled panic to see her controlled, distant demeanor. He wanted her passion. Her eager to wed him. Where was the woman from a few days ago?

When she reached his side, her hand shook as she held it out for him to clasp hers.

"Everything will be all right, love. We are together now." Even though she acknowledged his words with a subtle nod, he yearned for a smile. For a teasing glint in her eyes. For anything other than the sense she married out of duty. Or desperation.

He turned to face the preacher's kind countenance as the word *desperation* reverberated in his mind. How had it come to this? Had he been duped by a pretty face? Was he a fool to fall for the damsel in distress?

Charlotte stood surrounded by MacKinnon women, as her reception occurred around her. Even though they'd had short notice, the Odd Fellows Hall had been decorated for their wedding, and the townsfolk had been eager for another party. Charlotte forced a smile and laughter as the MacKinnon women teased her, but she saw their shared glances of concern at her feigned vivaciousness.

Resolutely refusing to answer any questions, she moved away from them to speak with a man called Bears. He had surprised her this morning with a beautiful bouquet of the yellow flowers she adored, telling her that he broke one of his rules by picking any of them just for her.

"Mr. Bears," she said, as she approached him. He was a tall, lean man with long black hair that hung loose down his back. His brown eyes shone with a quiet intelligence, and, although he focused solely on her, she had the sense he knew everything occurring in the Hall.

"It's just Bears, Missus," he said with a smile, his white teeth flashing. The red of his shirt enhanced the beauty of his light-brown skin, heralding his half–Native American heritage.

"I wanted to thank you again for the flowers."

He stared at her, as though understanding she wished to say more. When she remained quiet, he said, "I know many would have picked you twice as many flowers. But they will wilt soon enough, and we must leave flowers to seed for next year."

She nodded. "I have no complaint about the quantity." She shifted from foot to foot. "What did you mean about the preacher's blessing last night?" she asked. When he continued to stare at her with a patient understanding, she blurted out, "What more would I want than the preacher's blessing?"

He smiled then and nodded. "What more, indeed?" He motioned to the group gathered here. "Look around at the room, Missus. Everyone worked hard to ensure you had a wonderful day."

"No," she blurted out. "They worked hard for Dalton. They esteem him." She flushed. "I've done nothing to deserve ..." Her words sputtered to a halt, and she lowered her head.

"*Deserve*," he murmured. "If I were you, I'd examine what that word means to you. And the hold it has over your ability to find happiness."

Her head jerked up, as she stared at him in bewilderment. "What do you mean?"

Rather than expound on his idea, he stood quietly beside her, sipping a cup of overly sweetened punch for long moments. Finally he spoke in a low voice. "Do you believe a man cares for frilly things hanging from a ceiling? Or if the fine layer of dust has been swept from the floor of the Hall?" He shrugged. "We notice such things, but, for most of us, they won't enhance or hinder our ability to enjoy ourselves."

He looked at the bright room, filled with decorations, and recently scrubbed to a sparkling clean. "All of this, except for the cake and music, was done for you. I happen to know most men of the family are very partial to Anna's cakes." He winked at her. "And I've yet to meet a man who doesn't like holding his woman in his arms for a dance." He nodded in Dalton's direction, smiling. "Your husband already wants to waltz with you."

"I ... I can't imagine dancing in front of all these people," she sputtered, flushing when she saw an expectant look in her husband's gaze.

"It seems you are wanted, Missus. Needed." He paused as he gazed deeply into her eyes. "One day you will understand just how much you value being needed. For when he doesn't need you, you will have lost something precious. Something you may never recover again."

"I don't understand," she murmured, glancing around the room in dawning horror rather than in appreciation. She latched onto the town's kindness toward her, rather than the longing she had seen in her husband's gaze. "I ... I'll never be able to repay the townsfolk. I don't know what to do."

Placing a gentle hand on her arm, he gazed into her eyes. "They don't want anythin', Missus. A simple thank-you will suffice."

"That's never enough!" she cried out, as she raced from the room.

Frederick slapped Dalton on his shoulder, giving it a good squeeze. He followed the cowboy's gaze. "It seems she's enjoying her conversation with Bears."

"Or he's talking in circles again and confusing her when she needs clarity," Dalton said with a shake of his head, focusing on his boss and good friend. Dalton hoped his wife would overcome her shyness and come to him. Display some outward sign of joy that they were married.

Frederick rocked his head back and forth. "Have patience, and you'll see that everything will turn out well. She may be ... cautious right now. But she won't stay that way. Give her time."

"How much time did you give Miss Sorcha?" Dalton countered.

"Well, you know as well as I do that we'd been courtin', in our roundabout fashion, for a few years." He chuckled. "We were both impatient by the time the wedding night arrived." He stared with solemn sincerity at his friend. "Don't compare yourself with others, as that will only drive you mad. Find contentment with your own situation as it is."

After Dalton stewed a few moments on that comment, Frederick said, "Now, when we return to the ranch, I want you and your bride to head to the Henderson's."

Dalton forgot about his growing concern with Charlotte for a moment. "Why?" He stared at the ranch hands, coaxing women onto the dance floor, and smiled when he saw Shorty dancing with the pastor's sister. "Why wouldn't we remain near the big house with so many around to ensure Charlotte is safe?"

Frederick rubbed at his temple. "Well, that's just it. I think you need time away as a couple. And she'll be safe out at the distant homestead. No one will know where you are, except for a handful of us." He paused as he looked at Charlotte. "I think you need time alone, away from Sorcha and Davina. Away from the men."

"It's our busy time, Boss," Dalton protested.

"If you're feeling guilty, you can dig some post holes," he said with a smile and a laugh, slapping Dalton on the back again. "You only get one honeymoon. Enjoy it."

"A honeymoon," Dalton murmured, as he stared at his bride. "Thank you, Boss." He followed Frederick to join the MacKinnon men, Warren, and Ben, as they discussed the town. Although Dalton's gaze continually flicked to his wife, he attempted to focus on their conversation about the new schoolteacher hired for the next year, the controversy about ranchers fencing so much of the rangeland, and the speculation that the Montana Territory would finally become a state.

"How do you know this teacher will be any better than the last?" Dalton asked, as he attempted to focus on anything other than how his bride ignored him.

Warren, who was a member of the Town Improvement Committee and also partially responsible for finding the town's teacher, said, "I can't make any promises, but her references and qualifications are far superior to those of Mr. Danforth. It's a pity we've been without a teacher for a year, but I'm certain this new teacher will inspire our students. I believe she will be like Leticia."

Alistair, the second-eldest MacKinnon, smiled at that comment. "No one will ever compare to my Leticia." He glanced at his wife, chatting with the other MacKinnon women. Leticia had taught the children of Bear Grass Springs for years before she had married Alistair.

Warren chuckled. "Of course not. But we've chosen a … more mature teacher, and I hope that she will teach for many years here. Like Leticia." He focused on Alistair. "It's a pity you left the committee, although Ben's done an admirable job in your stead."

Alistair shrugged. "Ye ken I want as much time with my family as possible." He looked at Dalton. "Fetch yer bride. We all want cake."

Dalton nodded and searched for Charlotte. However, she was nowhere in sight. He approached Bears, who stood with his son, Jack, in his arms. "Bears, where's my wife?"

Bears stared at him in quiet commiseration. "She needed a moment." Shaking his head, he lowered his mouth to kiss his son's brow. "I wouldn't seek her out. She's muddled and needs to find her own way. Whatever you need to do, ask Anna to do it. She'll smooth it over, and no one will care."

Dalton stared dully at the MacKinnons, watching their conversation with avid interest. "I care," he whispered.

Bears nodded. "Show her that, Dalton. Be patient and

kind, as you always are. Find a way to prove to her that the man she married, that the man she trusts, isn't intent on acting like Warren's cousin." He paused and shook his head.

"No, tell me more. You clearly have opinions about her. Any of your wisdom is welcome, Bears. She doesn't want my company." He waved around, indicating her absence from their wedding reception.

"Oh, I think she does, but she doesn't believe she should." He rocked on his feet, soothing his son with his motion and with his calm voice. "She has odd notions. About who she is. What she owes others." He shrugged. "Be patient."

With a resolute sigh, Dalton approached Anna and the flock of women standing near his wedding cake. Speaking in a low voice, he murmured, "Anna, will you cut the cake with no fuss? I can't find Charlotte, and I don't want there to be talk."

Anna gaped at him before nodding. "Of course, Dalton." She motioned for Leticia, Fidelia, and Jane to follow her, and soon the beautiful cake had been sliced up with no fanfare and set out for the townsfolk to devour.

Sorcha sidled up to Dalton, little Harold in her arms. "Here," she murmured, thrusting the toddler into his hold. She shook her head when he would have protested. "Sometimes all we need are a few moments with a bairn to make the world right again." She stroked a hand down his shoulder before motioning Davina to join her in the front. Soon their voices filled the Odd Fellows Hall, and few of the townsfolk had an inclination to wonder why the happy couple hadn't cut the cake together. The crowd was too busily transfixed by the cousins' beautiful voices.

Frederick approached Dalton, a tender expression on his face, as he saw his friend holding his son. "That's Sorcha's gift to you," he murmured. "She'd never want you to suffer the town's censure as she did. As we did."

Dalton nodded, although he knew the true gift was having time with little Harold. For now he knew he had to have the courage to rekindle the deepest hope in his heart.

CHAPTER 11

D alton paced the small space in the room beside the bakery. Although June, the evening remained cool, and he lit a small fire in the potbellied stove. Anything to keep his mind off the disastrous wedding ceremony and the mockery of a wedding celebration. Anna had warned him that, although she rarely opened on a Sunday, she would open for limited hours tomorrow because the bakery had been closed since Wednesday, and too many townsfolk had complained that they needed bread.

"Not even my wedding night will be uninterrupted," he muttered. He kicked at a piece of wood in frustration, as he stared at the sleeping space, now covered by a curtain. Although it appeared a door might have been there at one time, a curtain separated the space large enough for a double bed from the room he was in, which had a crib, a rocking chair, a comfortable chair, and a potbellied stove.

When Charlotte remained hidden behind the curtain, Dalton spun and moved into the kitchen, where Anna had left a few plates of food and slabs of wedding cake. He hadn't eaten much since yesterday, and he was suddenly starving.

As he surveyed the small bounty of food, he felt guilty for excluding Charlotte. Poking his head back into the side room, he called out, "I'm eating dinner, if you want to join me." When silence was her response, he moved into the kitchen, rummaging around until he found a plate, silverware, and a glass.

He decided to sample everything, and he demolished half the food in quick succession. Arching his stomach out, he rubbed at his belly as he stared at the cake. One of his fondest wishes was to eat it with Charlotte. With another glance in the direction of the room his wife hid in, he tried first a bite of vanilla cake and then chocolate. "Oh, heaven," he sighed, as he ate the chocolate. "I wonder if Anna would make us one to take home."

He set down his fork with a clatter at the thought of returning to the home he'd shared with Mary. The home that had known so much harmony and passion and joy. How was he to live there with Charlotte with such friction between them? He rubbed at his head, wishing he knew what had caused her to change.

With a sigh, he rose. He had no desire to sleep in a chair on his wedding night. On cautious feet, he pushed open the curtain and poked his head in. "Lottie?" Even though he sensed she tried not to show any reaction to his presence, she stiffened. "Please stop ignoring me."

At the sound of her quiet sobbing, he sat on the bed, rubbing his hands over her back. "Is it that awful?" he whispered. "Being married to me?"

"No," she cried. "I … I don't think I'm ready for … for more than friendship."

Sighing, Dalton pinched the bridge of his nose. "That's fine."

"It is?" she asked, rolling onto her back to face him. Her eyes shone in the faint light from the other room, filled with shock and disappointment. "I thought you'd at least try to convince me."

"Oh, for God's sake," he muttered. "I've never been any good with riddles. I'm a basic man, Lottie. Either you want me or you don't. It's that simple."

"Nothing is that simple." She clamped her jaw shut, after snapping at him.

He leaned forward, tracing a finger over her soft cheek, frowning when she froze, after enjoying his gentle caress for a few moments. "What happened to make you change? Why don't you like my touch anymore?" He gazed into her eyes, as something that had been said to him today tickled his memory. "Who spoke venom to you?" He waited for her to say something, shaking his head in disappointment when she remained quiet. "Why won't you tell me? I'm your husband. I will honor you in all things."

"I can't tell you because I don't know," she said. "I …" She looked at him, her hand raising to play through his brown hair, before she snatched it down. "I don't know what to do. How to act."

At her plaintive wail, Dalton smiled. "You don't have to act or do anything, Lottie. Just be. Just feel." He paused. as he ran a soothing hand over her arm. "What do you want?"

"I want our marriage to be real," she whispered. Her next words extinguished his burgeoning hope. "Our marriage isn't binding until … until …" She shrugged and flushed.

"Until we make love?" He nodded. "I suppose that's true. But I'd challenge any man who dared think he could take you from me." He paused. "As long as I knew you wanted to be by my side." When his words caused fresh tears to well in her eyes, he shook his head. "I don't understand you. You don't want my touch. You're only concerned that our wedding be binding but not because of any true regard for me."

He rose, pacing a step away before sitting again, this time

not touching her. "You didn't want me near you after the wedding. You disappeared when it was time for our dance, and we never cut the cake together."

Closing her eyes, she shrugged. "You should have your memories from your first wedding. Guard those."

Dalton jerked back, his heart bruised. "I wanted them with you, Lottie, and you stole them from me. What else will you steal, now that we are married?" He moved to rise again, stilling his movement when she grabbed at his hand.

"No. Stay," she entreated. "I ... Please."

He froze, muscles bunched tight, as though fighting his instinct to leap away from her. "This is our wedding night, Lottie. If I remain, I can't promise what won't happen." He waited, his breath leaving in a *whoosh* when she flipped up the blankets, inviting him into bed with her. He took a deep breath and rose, stripping off his outer clothes. "I'll join you, love. And pray you won't come to resent me too."

Dalton stood at the paddock railing, watching as Bears worked a horse with Davina. He recalled Slims's mention of his wife's fascination with horses, and Dalton knew this was one way his foreman could show support to his wife. Dalton nodded to Slims, as the giant of a man approached with a cup of coffee.

"Have you had a cup of Anna's coffee?" Slims asked. "You won't have better in the Territory."

"Don't let Miss Irene hear you say that," Dalton said with a smile. "Yes, I've had two already today."

Shaking his head, Slims stared at him a long moment, before focusing on his wife. "Ah, there's a joyful sight," he murmured with pride.

"She's keen."

"Aye," Slims said. "More keen than you appeared to be to remain in your bride's bed." He watched his friend over the edge of his coffee mug, as he took another sip. "If I had time away from the duties of the ranch, I'd take advantage of every moment."

"It takes two to be eager," Dalton muttered. He shook his head ruefully at Slims's shocked expression.

Taking two large swallows of coffee, Slims set down the mug and slung his arms over the paddock pole, mimicking Dalton's stance. He bent down, so they were eye to eye, speaking in a low voice, so the conversation was solely for them. "What happened? I thought you would be happy with her. Like you were with your Mary."

Dalton shifted. "I think I expected too much, Slims. I thought we'd have what you and Davina have. Or share what Boss and Miss Sorcha do."

"And you don't?" Slims asked with furrowed brow. "You're the only man she ever wants near her. You're the only man she relaxes around." He shook his head, as though it were a puzzle he couldn't decipher.

"It's nothing," Dalton said. "It'll resolve."

Slims snorted and shook his head. "Now I know you're an idiot. Nothing ever resolves with a woman without talkin' about it. That's one thing I've learned. Besides, if you've got doubts, she'll sense somethin's wrong, and you'll push her even farther away. Talk to her, Dalt." Slims stepped away, calling out encouraging words to Davina, moving to intercept Shorty and Dixon, so as to gift Dalton more time alone.

Dalton stood, staring into space, as he considered the previous night. He had promised himself nothing more than cuddling would happen. But then she had turned, pressing against him. Somehow they had begun to kiss. Long passionate kisses. Soft caresses turning into so much more. He clung to the memory of her whispering *yes* over

147

and over again. Of the desire he thought he'd seen in her eyes.

Although there had been passion, he realized he had yearned for so much more. Joy and laughter and the sense she felt the same sense of wonder as he did. That she marveled at her good fortune and gave thanks to be in his arms, as he gave thanks he had been blessed that she chose him. Instead he had felt a chasm growing between them.

Rather than holding her in his arms, he had let her sleep apart, as she claimed she wanted. Rather than breathe in the subtle scent of her hair and feel its silkiness tickle his nose as he woke up, he had to settle for the dream of what might come. Rather than feel her stretch and arch up to kiss his cheek and to scrub her fingers over his stubble, he had to accept her tumbling out of bed to hastily change and scurry away.

He bowed his head, rubbing at his hair, as he fought doubts. Mary had never seemed dissatisfied by his lovemaking, but then she'd never had another lover. Perhaps Charlotte compared him to Warren's cousin and realized all she was missing. All she had given up by marrying Dalton. He let out a deep breath, as doubt took root deep in his soul. A doubt he feared he could never banish.

Charlotte sat at the counter in the bakery, watching as Annabelle measured flour and sugar for a cake. Fidelia washed dishes, while Jane tended the front. Jessamine had just poked her head in, seemingly delighted to have a large group of women to chat with.

Jessamine stared at Charlotte with her reporter's assessing look, her hand lazily stroking Aileana's back. "You don't look like a blushing bride the morning after. You look like you're on the verge of attending a funeral."

"Jessamine!" Annabelle scolded. "Hush."

"Well, someone needs to say it," Jessamine said, pushing back a lock of her red hair, as she raised an eyebrow, daring anyone to contradict her assessment. When no one did, she gave a small huff of satisfaction. "See? You all agree. You're just too polite to say anything. Then she'd leave, and we'd have no idea what the strife was about."

"There is no strife," Charlotte protested. "And I have no interest in being in your newspaper."

Jessamine laughed, settling into a rocking chair in the corner. "I fear you will be disappointed on that score. You will be alluded to, as I discuss Warren's horrible cousin. It can't be helped." She smiled. "But I have no desire to talk about anyone's wedding night in my paper. That is far too personal." Her cognac-colored eyes glowed with mischievousness. "However, not so personal you can't talk with us about it."

Against her will, Charlotte giggled. "You are as incorrigible as your husband." When that comment made Jessamine beam, Charlotte shook her head. "I'd thought you'd be chagrined."

"Why should I be embarrassed by the truth?" Jessamine asked, as she shrugged. "We are who we are, and we accept ourselves." She smiled broadly, as Sorcha emerged from the back room, tiptoeing as she shut the door.

"The wee beasts are down for their naps," she said with a smile and a sigh. She collapsed in the other rocking chair. "So, are we finally talking about Charlotte's disastrous weddin' night?"

Gaping at everyone present, Charlotte sputtered, "How? How do you know it's disastrous?"

"Well, ye're out here with us, rather than sequestered in

there with him," Sorcha said with a wave of her hand to indicate the bed in the other room.

"I'd never stay abed when others were nearby. Or when work was to be done," Charlotte said, her cheeks reddening.

"Ah, you must overcome your reticence," Fidelia said. "And I don't say that as a former Boudoir Beauty. I say that as a woman who loves a man but has two children. If you worry about others being in the house, you'll never have time for you and your husband." She saw the other women smile and nod. "As long as you have a closed door, and you know you won't be interrupted, enjoy the time you have with your husband."

"I think 'tis more than just this mornin'," Sorcha said. "Were ye disappointed in the man?"

"No," Charlotte gasped. "No," she said again, suddenly fighting tears. "I … I fear he was wishing it were Mary in his arms. Mary, who knew what he liked. Not some woman with little experience, who threw away her innocence on a worthless man." She sniffled.

Annabelle cast a glance around the room, before setting aside the mixing bowl. "If that's how you felt last night, it's no wonder you're sitting here, looking morose and confused." She moved around the kitchen island and wrapped an arm around Charlotte's shoulder. "The first question I have for you is, are you all right?"

Charlotte furrowed her brows, as she gazed into Annabelle's worried eyes. "All right?" Her eyes rounded, and then she blushed in mortification. "Of course I am! He's a wonderful man." She ignored the other women in the room, listening to their conversation, and focused on Annabelle.

"If he's wonderful, what happened?" Annabelle asked, her voice kind and understanding. Like a doting mother's voice. A loving sister's voice.

Charlotte's eyes filled. "I've never had this," she whispered. "I've never known such kinship."

Annabelle smiled, squeezing her arm. "Well, I'm afraid you're stuck with us. You're one of us now." She waited patiently for Charlotte to speak.

"I ... I felt so inept. I didn't know what to do. And he was so kind and patient, but I didn't know if I could ask if he enjoyed himself." She closed her eyes, flushing beet red, as she ducked her head. "What if he said he hadn't? Or I could tell he lied as he tried to protect my feelings?"

"Oh, Charlotte," Annabelle murmured, as she tugged her into her embrace. "We all feel inept and inadequate at some point. But nothing ever improves if we don't talk. You have to speak with him."

"How?" Charlotte cried out, her hand waving in the air. "I can't just blurt it out now, asking him if he enjoyed himself."

Fidelia approached and spoke in a quiet voice. "I think you might need to." When she saw Charlotte's instinctual shake of her head in denial, Fidelia said, "I worried Bears would believe I was comparing him to every man who had joined me at the Boudoir." Her innate vitality dimmed as she spoke of her time at the town's brothel. "I needed to reassure him that, when I was with him, the only man I thought of was my husband. It was a gift to him but also to myself."

Charlotte stared at her in confusion. "Why for both of you?"

"By alleviating his fears, it allowed both of us to be free of the restraints of our pasts. It showed my trust in him." She smiled, her eyes now glowing as she talked about her husband. "I won't lie and say it was easy. It was very hard. I had nightmares to overcome, but I learned to relish sleeping in Bears's arms."

"I pushed him away last night, after we ... we ..." Charlotte motioned with her arm. "He wanted to hold me close.

I've never been held like that after … after … and I was afraid. It's so different when you're not wearing clothes." She broke off what more she would have said, afraid the women would laugh at her naive statement. At the deafening silence in the room, she blurted out, "I didn't want to give him every part of me."

"Oh, Charlotte," Sorcha said, as she rose, enfolding her in a fierce hug. "Ye have it all backward, lass. Ye give every part of yerself so that he will do the same. Ye are no' losin' yourself. Ye're gainin' everythin'. A true partnership. A husband who would walk through fire for ye."

Charlotte looked around at the women gathered in the room, her gaze shrouded. "I don't know how to be brave, like all of you. I don't have your courage."

"Hogwash," Jane said. She stepped forward. "I understand what you're feeling. You're an outsider, like I was when I first arrived. Before I accepted my place in the family. The difference is, you aren't tied to the women here by blood of any kind. But that doesn't mean the offer of kinship is any less sincere."

Jane looked at her family. At their subtle nods, she said, "All of us have had to face our deepest fears. Annabelle had to face losing Cailean, if she didn't learn to trust him again after a horrible betrayal. Jessamine had to overcome fears of infertility. Sorcha worried none could truly love her because the woman who raised her was cruel and resented her. Fidelia thought herself unworthy after working at the Boudoir. I'd had a failed relationship with a mean man who tried to destroy my spirit. And my own father nearly broke my heart." She shook her head, clearing her eyes of tears that threatened to fall from the memory of those days. "But, through it all, we found the strength to believe. To trust. And to love. As you must."

"I don't know if I can," she whispered.

"If ye dinna, then ye will lose him," Sorcha whispered, her gaze sorrowful. "An' that would be the greatest misfortune of all."

"Believe what you know to be true here," Fidelia murmured, pointing to her chest and alluding to her heart, "not the lies someone has fed you. Too often I believed the falsehoods peddled by someone intent on using and abusing me. Don't give anyone that power over you."

Charlotte sighed, resting her head against Annabelle's shoulder, feeling safe and secure for the moment, although her mind raced at the prospect of being as brave as the women so effortlessly offering her kinship.

~

Charlotte stiffened as she approached the wagon. Smiling bravely at Dalton, she saw him speaking with Adella, and Charlotte wished she could run and hide. Instead she firmed her shoulders and approached her husband. "Hello," she murmured, standing beside him.

"Love," he said, reaching for her hand and lacing their fingers together. "We have a farewell committee." His blue eyes sparkled with mischief as he looked at her, causing her to relax against him.

"I'll never believe you truly wanted to marry this imposter," Adella hissed. "She's duped you!"

Dalton took a deep breath, his hand tightening its hold on Charlotte's. "Ma'am, I'd watch how you speak about my wife." Although outwardly friendly, his blue eyes had turned glacially cold, and he stared at Adella with lethal hatred. "I fear we have a different definition of trickery. I would consider the ultimate deception to be a woman of society inviting an innocent woman for a visit and serving her a tea that would lead to the loss of her child."

Adella scoffed. "Is that what she told you?" She rolled her eyes. "Why would I deign to hurt her when I wanted to raise the child myself?" She looked over Charlotte in her green calico dress with unconcealed loathing. "Every man wanders, dear. You'll discover that soon enough." She focused on Dalton again. "She should have agreed to give me the child, rather than drag you into some elaborate farce, after she suffered from her attempt to rid herself of the brat growing in her belly."

Charlotte turned, ignoring Adella. "I swear it's as I said, Dalton. There were two teapots. She didn't drink what I did." When he stared at her with an implacable gaze, she whispered, "Please."

He blinked once and focused again on the woman who had harmed his wife. "Tell me, Mrs. Coldwell. I never did ascertain the reason for your arrival to our small town." He ignored the fact that two McLeod brothers, plus Warren, Frederick, and Bears all loitered behind Adella, blatantly listening in.

"Why, when I learned my dear Orville's cousin lived in this godforsaken territory too, I knew I needed to do my Christian duty and visit him. And urge him to consider moving to Butte to live near us. Family must always stick together."

"Is that so?" Warren said in a low voice. "Is that why I hadn't seen you once in the two weeks since your arrival until last night? I find that Orville's side of the family only ever cared to seek me out when he needed help with a legal matter. Otherwise, they never had much use for me. I wasn't entertaining enough for them."

Adella gasped, as she spun around to face the men behind her. "You are uncouth men, listening in on a conversation that doesn't pertain to you."

"Oh, but it does, ma'am," Frederick said with a mocking

bow of his head. "Dalton's one of us. You hurt him, or his wife, and you've harmed us. It's as simple as that." He smiled when she stared at him, as though he had the logic of a fool hen.

"Well, I fear you've been taken in by a charlatan. No matter what she's told you, she desired my husband's attentions." She spoke in a loud carrying voice, smiling as a few of the passing townsfolk stumbled when they walked past. "She does not know the meaning of the words loyalty or fidelity. It would be better for all if she were to return to Butte with me."

Dalton tilted his head. "Because you are so familiar with those sentiments?"

Adella preened at him, delighted that he was more quick witted than she assumed a cowpoke would be.

Charlotte stood beside her husband, quivering, as everyone spoke around her, as though she weren't here. As though everything she had related had been a figment of her imagination. "No," she whispered. "I will never return to Butte. If I do, you'll find a way to hurt me. To …"

Adella stared at her with patent pity. "My dear, why would I do any such thing? You know we want to make amends for what occurred. We were eager to offer you a position in our home as a maid." She brightened. "Or a cook. I hear you are quite adept at that trade."

Warren studied her. "Charlotte's a married woman. Inform Orville she's beyond your sphere of influence." His gaze hardened. "And don't imagine the pastor will take your interference in his proceedings in this town lightly. He's an upstanding man of the cloth."

"Oh, I'm certain Pastor Cruikshanks can be persuaded to see the benefit of looking the other way. He's always been a reasonable man."

"You know him?" Cailean asked. At her satisfied smile,

Cailean grinned. "Then 'tis my pleasure to inform you that he left town. In February. We have a new pastor, and he's a good man." His smile broadened when she paled.

Dalton finally spoke, in a low ire-filled voice. "I've had enough, Mrs. Coldwell. You disparage me and the sanctity of the vows I took yesterday when I married my wife. I was not coerced. I was not bamboozled. I was not so out of my mind with lust that I didn't know what I was doing." He glared the woman into silence, as he released Charlotte's hand and wrapped his arm around his wife's waist, hauling her against his side. "I married her knowing everything she suffered at the hands of your husband. Fully understanding your part in her pain. I will never allow you to harm her again."

"Surely you can see the benefit to looking the other way?" Adella said. "Financial compensations—"

"I don't want money!" Dalton roared. "I don't want anything but her," he said next, in a near whisper, all the more powerful for the fierce emotion lacing his voice. "Leave our town and never return. You are not welcome here."

"Aye," Ewan said, as he sauntered up to them. "An' I ken Jessie is writin' a tremendous article about the interloper from Butte. Should be somethin' to read. Perhaps she'll send it along to one of the papers in Butte?"

Adella paled. "She wouldn't! You wouldn't!" She spun to gaze imploringly at Warren.

"Jessie's her own woman. She'll do what she sees fit. And I'd never interrupt her in this endeavor, for it seems just to me."

"Vile heathens," she rasped, as she glared at them. "I warned Orville that we should never leave Philadelphia." With that, she spun on her heel to march away.

Charlotte let out a sputtering breath, as she watched Adella walk in the direction of the hotel. Dalton eased his hold on her, and she whimpered, "No, please hold me."

He stilled, his muscles tight with tension. "You can't have it both ways, Lottie." After an agonizingly long moment, he pulled her close. "*Shh*, love, you're all right. You're fine." When tears soaked his shirt, he groaned. "Don't cry so, love. She's not worth your emotions."

Frederick approached the couple and sighed. "So much for having a wedding and starting a marriage without scandal. I'm certain this encounter is now the most-talked-about episode in town in recent months." He patted Dalton on his shoulder, as he soothed Charlotte, and Frederick moved away.

"I'm sorry," she stammered against his chest. "I knew better than to accept your proposal. I knew I'd bring you nothing but problems."

He shook his head. "No, Lottie. This is nothing. Defending you from that viper was a pleasure." He released her and backed away a step. "Living without your regard? Without your desire for true intimacy? *That* is what I mourn." He gave a brisk nod and left her to join the men in readying the wagons.

"Dalton," she whispered, watching him leave her behind, when she still yearned for his arms around her. Was this how he'd felt last night, when she'd spurned his touch? When she insisted on sleeping alone on the edge of the bed, wrapped up in a blanket, so he wouldn't touch her? She rubbed at her head, overcome with the sense she had just lost something precious.

CHAPTER 12

Charlotte sat beside Dalton, the ranch behind them. With the long June nights, he had said they would arrive at the Henderson homestead in an hour or so, just in time for a cold supper. She gazed at the mountains, subtly glowing in the early evening light. Little snow remained on the peaks, and the lush green of previous weeks had already faded to a dull dun color.

After an hour of silence, Dalton said, "Tell me the true reason that woman came to town."

Charlotte jerked at the harsh tone in his voice. "I'm confused by all she said to me. She claims she wanted to convince me to give her my baby."

Dalton frowned, his gaze on the horses and the faint wagon ruts in front of him. "Which means, she didn't give you tea to cause you to lose your baby, if she came to town believin' you were still with child." His fingers tightened on the horse's reins, causing the horses to toss their heads as though they sensed his tension. "Why make up such a story?"

"I didn't! I swear," she gasped. Her hands covered her belly in a protective manner. When they hit a jarring rut, one hand flew out to grab the seat, so she wouldn't bounce off. She gazed at the rangeland, but she saw those disjointed moments in Butte, when all she knew was fear and betrayal and heartbreak. "I was told. By Orville. As I left the house. That she had tricked me. That I was a naive fool for accepting tea with her because she was vindictive and cruel and always treated his … lovers in such a way."

"Orville," he spat. His shoulders slunk lower, as he curled into himself. "Do you still dream of him?"

"What?" Charlotte gasped, her eyes rounded in horror. "How can you ask me that when you know all I suffered at his hands?"

Staring defiantly ahead, Dalton said, "I refuse to explain the obvious, Charlotte." After a long moment of silence, he muttered, "But I know it wasn't *my* touch you desired last night."

Silent tears coursed down her cheek, marring her view of the rolling hills and mountains, as they changed colors in the early evening light. "Now, now that we are married, you doubt me."

He pulled on the reins, stilling the steady progression of the horses. Tying up the reins, he hopped down and held his arms up for her. "Come, Lottie. We have to talk, and I don't want to do it where I can't look at you." After helping her down, he walked a short distance away, kicking rocks and tufts of dirt. "The problem, Lottie, is I don't know all you suffered at his hands. I need to hear it from you."

She stared at him in confusion. "Why? What good will it do for you to know about me being attacked and pulled into an alley to be beaten and left for dead?"

He swore and marched away a few paces, before letting out an anguished roar as he bent over at his waist. He stood tall again, his hands clenched together at his side, and he turned to face her, wearing a mask of rage. He held out a hand when she backed away a step. "No, love, forgive me." He closed his eyes, corralling his deep emotions. "None of this is for you. It's for that monster who ever dared hurt you." He swallowed, asking in a low voice, "Did Adella ask you about the baby when you had tea with her?"

Charlotte paled, her hands over her belly again. "Yes." She bit her lip, thinking over that distant memory. "She tried to convince me to live in Butte until I had the baby and to promise to leave once I did. When I spurned that offer, she was irate but insisted I remain for tea. Said she refused to have the servants spread gossip about her being a poor hostess."

Dalton scratched at his head, staring at the mountains. "Why would you believe Warren's cousin?" When he saw her pale, he asked, "Why wouldn't you believe he'd continue to lie to you?"

"Don't you understand? I needed to have faith someone cared for me. I was completely alone in this world, and he seemed genuinely concerned." Her mouth dropped open, and she gasped. "He asked me where I was staying, and I told him. I gave him the information he needed so his men could find me."

Dalton took a halting step toward her. "Did they strike you in your belly? Kick you?" At her swift nod, he closed his eyes, before taking the few steps that separated them and pulling her close. "I'm so sorry, love."

"Why?" she cried. "Why would he hurt me?"

He ran soft hands over her back. "I can't answer for Orville. I wouldn't want to have to answer for his sins." He sighed with pleasure when she clung to him and didn't fight being in his arms. "I promise you, Lottie. I will have faith in you. And I will not touch you again as a husband until I know it is what you truly want. You've had enough of having your choices taken from you."

"But—"

When he placed his fingers over her lips, she swallowed what more she would have said in protestation. Dalton shook his head to silence her. "No, I mean what I say, Lottie. I care for you, and I won't, ... I can't ..." He broke off, easing her away, as he smoothed tears off her cheeks with his fingers. "Come. We must continue on, if we are to arrive before nightfall."

Charlotte crawled back onto the wagon bench beside her husband, relieved the anger between them had been resolved. However, a different tension thrummed through her. So much remained unsettled. How was she to show her husband her desire without fear that he would pity her?

That evening set the tone for the next week. After emptying the wagon and stabling the horses, Dalton joined Charlotte in the kitchen for a simple supper. After a few minutes of awkward silence, their customary ease returned, and they chatted about their time in town. As it came time for bed, he waited for her to settle on her side, curled away from him, and he laid down with his back to her.

Although he thought he'd toss and turn and rue the fact his wife didn't want to be held by him, he slept soundly. As was his custom, he woke early and rose, leaving her slumbering beside him. After fixing a pot of coffee, he wandered outside to stare at the outbuildings. The chicken coop looked as though it would fall down with the next strong wind. The barn was in decent shape, although a few shingles were missing, and it needed patching in places.

After finishing his coffee, he set off in the direction of the barn to search out supplies he'd need to repair the barn.

When that was completed, he'd move to the chicken coop and digging post holes. Anything to occupy his time while out here alone with a wife who had no desire for his attention. His affection. His jaw tightened at the thought, and he forced himself to relax.

Closing his eyes, he reminded himself that he had to be patient to earn her trust. A deep yearning settled in his chest that he had been the one to travel here with Lottie last summer. That they had had the chance to fall in love then. That she had never known heartbreak and betrayal. For he feared he'd never prove himself worthy of her full regard. He ducked his head, rubbing at the back of his neck. He didn't know how he'd live years with only a sham of a marriage.

"Dalton?" her soft voice called out.

He spun to her. "Yes? Are you well, Lottie?" His eager gaze took in her mint-green calico dress, slightly wrinkled from all their recent travels.

"I … of course. Breakfast is ready. I can't imagine you'd be successful with your work if you haven't eaten." She looked at her feet. "You shouldn't have let me sleep. My job is to cook for you."

"Your job?" he whispered. "No, Lottie, you don't work for me. You're my wife." He shook his head with frustration. "You were exhausted after everything that's occurred recently. There was no reason for me to wake you." His hand rose to stroke her hair, but he stilled the motion when she flinched. "Lottie?"

"If I don't cook, what kind of wife am I?" she cried out. "You already made your own coffee. Did you eat too, and clean up after yourself?" By this point she was on the verge of hysteria.

"Lottie," he said in a calm voice. He gripped her arms, looking deeply into her eyes. "Love, please. I never meant to make you feel unworthy. I wanted to give you time to rest."

He paused before muttering, "I only wish I'd given you a reason to be exhausted this morning." He smiled with chagrin as she gaped at him, her beautiful sherry-colored eyes filled with embarrassment. "There's nothing wrong with a husband sayin' he desires his wife's company," he whispered, as he kissed her cheek. He sobered. "Please don't deny me the right to look after you, Lottie."

She swallowed, staring deeply into his gaze. "You were truly worried about me?" At his nod, she pressed forward into his arms. "I don't know how to do this," she cried out.

"This?" he said in a soft voice, wrapping his arms around her and breathing a sigh of relief to hold her in his arms again.

"Be a wife. Be what you want. I …I don't know what to do!"

He urged her back a step, so he could gaze into her eyes. "Neither do I. We'll learn together, Lottie. Form our own marriage. It's what you do with someone you care about." His fingers played through the hair framing her face and tickling down to her ear. "We'll have missteps and fights and misunderstandings. But let's try." He swallowed, as he was unable to hide the pleading in his voice.

"Yes," she whispered, "let's try." She kissed him on his jaw and clasped his hand. "Come, husband. It's time for breakfast. I want us to eat together every morning. I want it to be one of our traditions."

A satisfied smile bloomed. "I like the sound of that, Lottie. I want us to have traditions." He walked beside her into the homestead that already felt like a home, simply because of her presence.

A week later, Charlotte dug through the boxes of supplies Dixon had delivered an hour ago. He'd only stayed long enough to have a cup of coffee and a slice of her rhubarb cake before returning to the main ranch. Charlotte had thought he'd be a source of gossip, but he'd chattered on about the fence building and the unsuccessful search for another cook.

Although Charlotte relished her time with Dalton, an undercurrent of tension thrummed between them. They continued to sleep as though a chasm separated them, and at times she wished she could cuddle up against him. However, she didn't want to give him the wrong idea, and he always jerked like she'd poked him with a hot fire iron when she touched him. Biting her lip, she feared her touch evoked pain rather than pleasure.

She turned to the second box of supplies, stilling when she saw a newspaper on top and a few letters. Lifting the newspaper, she realized it was Jessamine's. Scanning the front-page story, she collapsed onto a nearby stool. "Oh my," she breathed, as her gaze raced over the article.

"Is everything all right, Lottie?" Dalton asked, earning a startled shriek from her as she dropped the newspaper to her lap.

"Dalton," she gasped.

"Who else would you be expectin'?" He tilted his head to the side, pointing to her lap. "What is that?"

"It's the newspaper. I'm so embarrassed," Lottie said, as her cheeks flamed. With reluctance, she handed it to Dalton, who sat across from her and read it aloud.

TRUE & TANTALIZING

It has come to my attention, dear reader, that we were graced by the presence of a woman of the finest society this past weekend. Our great misfortune is that we were unaware of such genteel breeding among us and were unable to proffer her the adulation she is accustomed to. Why one of purported good breeding, fine manners, and impeccable tastes would deign to visit our small town is a mystery. Her boorish manners, her impolitic comments, and her persistent refusal to dance led this observer to believe she was a crow in a peacock's dress. Perhaps I was mistaken.

Although claiming a friendship with one of our newest and most estimable residents, it remains doubtful she and Miss Ingram were ever more than acquaintances. After the visitor attempted to dig her talons into our estimable lawyer, Mr. Clark, he proclaimed that he had thought the interloper's natural habitat was one of soirees and balls. Preferably in Philadelphia. Not our town's joyous celebration of its founding.

I must admit that I watched the visitor with a morbid fascination. What sort of woman is intent on mischief and provoking discord between a man who desired to wed the woman he loved? What sort of woman continually attempts to sow strife between family and friends? Why would such a woman ever be someone to be emulated?

This woman, who by all appearances had everything she could ever want, had nothing. She lacked in everything that is truly precious. Love. Family. The esteem of those you cherish. She was a shell of what one should dream of becoming. The pursuit of the superficial had stripped her of life's true pleasures. And I pity her for that. My hope, dear reader, is that you have discovered that there is more to life than the next harvest, the next roundup, or finding the next gold nugget.

So much more.

As for our interloper, I saw her, with the greatest relief, depart town a few days after our town dance, fervently hopeful she will never flutter her overstarched silk skirts on our boardwalks again.

Dalton scratched at his head, as he stared at the paper. "I

like to think I can read, but what exactly did she say?" He looked to Charlotte in bewilderment with brows furrowed. "If I think too hard, I'll give myself a headache."

Charlotte laughed. "Oh, Dalton, thank you. I hate that Jessamine wrote about me—us—in an indirect way. That she alluded to the fact we're having trouble as a couple." She bit her lip, as though she had said too much, dropping her head down.

The paper rustled as Dalton set it down. "Are we, Lottie?" When she wouldn't look at him, he rasped, "Are we having trouble as a couple?" He rose and paced away. "I thought we were doing all right. We like each other. We always have something to converse about." He shrugged.

"Is that enough?" she whispered, daring to look at him.

He stood with his hands on his hips, staring out the window. "No. Never," he rasped. "But I'm patient. I'll wait." He looked at her. "You deserve that, Lottie." He nodded to the supplies. "I'm glad Fred sent out plenty. We'll be fine for another week or so." He spun on his heel and left.

"Dalt …" She bit her lip as the sound of his boot heels faded away. "How am I supposed to seduce a man when I have no idea about the art of seduction?" She dropped her head forward to rest on her folded arms. With aching clarity, she wished she were at the main ranch, with Sorcha and Davina near her. They would help her. They would have pushed her to do something days ago. For Charlotte feared, the longer she allowed insecurity and fear to limit her actions, the harder it would be to show her husband just how much she desired him.

CHAPTER 13

A week later, Charlotte stood on the stoop of the homestead's small front porch, wishing for something more to do. For some company. She had mended shirts, and she knew she could knit another pair of socks, but she had already knitted a half-dozen pair. Would her husband go through so many socks in one winter? With a sigh, she walked down the front steps, wishing Dalton were here. He'd ridden out a few hours ago to check on the cattle, although she suspected he needed a little time alone. He'd desired time alone every day since they had arrived a few weeks ago.

She refused to begrudge him that need, for she knew he relished his time riding the range. When he returned to the homestead, he'd have a tale for her. She'd laugh and enjoy their moments together, until the evening winded down. Then the tension and the stilted silences would begin. She only wished the distance that seemed to grow between them each night could be easily overcome. Her reticence at being touched while in bed had formed a wedge between them, and she didn't know how to span that gap. She wished she had the confidence to seduce him.

Closing her eyes, she recalled her attempt a few nights ago. She had played with the button on her dress, smiling in a welcoming manner. He had stared at her a long moment, a flush rising on his cheeks to the point she worried he was ailing with a summer fever. Suddenly he rose, marching to the door. *"I want a wife, Lottie, not a tease,"* he had rasped, before leaving and slamming the door behind him. His words echoed in her brain. The memory of him storming from their room replayed over and over again, as did the long night without the comfort of knowing he was near. For the first time since their wedding, he had slept somewhere other than their bed.

Covering her eyes with the palm of one hand, she looked out at the flat land, leading in the direction of the mountains. Although she'd promised her husband she'd always keep the homestead within view, she could walk a fair distance without breaking that promise.

She saw a movement in a nearby field, and her curiosity was piqued. Walking with purposeful strides, she made her way across the uneven ground, each footstep causing a small puff of dirt to rise. "How quickly it dries out," she murmured. Glancing over her shoulder, she saw the far outline of the homestead and knew she needed to stop.

However, when she faced forward, she saw a beautiful chestnut-colored stallion with its mane billowing in the breeze. Her breath caught as he turned to stare at her, his nostrils flaring, as though he caught her scent. He reared, running toward her for a few strides before veering away.

Charlotte held a hand to her chest, collapsing to her knees. "Oh, good Lord," she whispered. "He could have trampled me." She looked up to see the horse watching her. He tossed his head and took a few steps, as though urging her to follow him. She shook her head, backing away, so that she continued to face him. "No, beauty," she called out. "I must return home."

She smiled as the horse neighed and trotted away in the opposite direction, watching the stallion's fluid, graceful movements. "I wonder why he's not one of Frederick's horses."

Charlotte retraced her path home, her mind filled with possibilities.

Days later, Charlotte exclaimed, "Mr. Dixon!" as she returned to the homestead after her now daily walk to meet with the wild stallion. "What a surprise." She flushed as he looked her over from head to foot and frowned. "I wasn't expecting you."

"Were you expectin' someone else?" he asked with a sharp tilt of his head, his gaze penetrating and none of his customary teasing present in his expression.

"Of course not," she sputtered. Wrapping an arm around her waist, she remained outside with him. "I'm afraid my husband is out on the range today. I'm uncertain when he'll return."

Dixon nodded, taking off his hat to tap against his thigh. "I've stabled my horse. I can wait."

Charlotte blushed and battled her inclination to stomp her foot in frustration at his tone—implying she had been caught doing something wrong. "I would prefer you remain outside until my husband returns. If you are thirsty, a stream is nearby." She waved in the direction of the creek. She clomped inside, slamming the door behind her. This was the first time she'd been so uncharitable to him, but she had no desire for his rude company.

Taking deep breaths, Charlotte forced herself to calm

down. Until now, Dixon had always been friendly, even mildly flirtatious. Today he had looked at her with suspicion. With a shiver, she realized how much she had relied on the trust everyone had shown her since she had revealed her past. To have anyone doubt her now provoked pain and confusion. What could have happened?

With quivering legs, Charlotte forced herself to move to the room she shared with Dalton to wash the dirt off her face and neck. Rather than lay down for the nap she desperately desired, she moved to the kitchen to prepare supper. Looking out the window, she saw Dixon sitting on a stump of wood. "Did you bring supplies?" she called out the window.

"No," he yelled back. "Boss didn't think you'd be needin' 'em."

"That's odd," Charlotte muttered under her breath. She looked around at their paltry stores. Nearly out of flour, sugar, and all other baking necessities, they would either need to be replaced by a delivery from the main ranch, or she and Dalton would have to return. Tonight would be another basic meal of stew and day-old bread without butter.

After a few hours puttering around the kitchen and daydreaming, she looked out the window to see Dalton chatting with Dixon in a low voice. Whatever the younger man said to her husband infuriated him, as he glowered and spun away to kick at a clump of dirt. When the words "impropriety" and "shame" carried on the faint breeze, she shivered and backed away from the kitchen window. Soon enough she would learn the reason behind Dixon's visit.

D alton wolfed down his wife's stew, barely tasting it. When his bowl was empty, he waved away her offer for a second helping. Waiting for Dixon to finish eating, Dalton cleared his throat when the younger man gave him a subtle nod. "Charlotte, there's something we must—I must—talk with you about."

Her spoon dropped into her bowl with a clatter. "What is it?" she whispered. Her gaze moved between the two men, before focusing on her husband. "Please, just tell me."

"I don't know if I told you, but, when we were in town for our wedding, it was decided that we would pool our resources so that we knew where Orville was at all times."

She paled, shaking her head. "No, you didn't tell me any of that," she whispered. "And we don't have the money for that."

He sighed, reaching for her hands. "I know. But our ... friends are very generous. They want to ensure your safety."

"They consider you family, Missus," Dixon said stiffly.

"What's happened?" Charlotte asked, her attention wholly focused on her husband. "Why did Mr. Dixon need to visit us on our honeymoon if not to bring us supplies?"

Dalton let out a breath and swore softly. "That's just the thing, Lottie. This isn't simply our honeymoon. We came here to hide away a while. To make sure the danger to you had passed." He held on to her hands, when she would have pulled them away. "And I'm afraid it hasn't."

"You're speaking in riddles, Dalton," she whispered. "How could I be in danger out here? No one knows where I am."

Flushing, Dixon moved his head in an apologetic manner. "You're not completely correct in that. All of the ranch knows. All the MacKinnons and their friends know. And Mr. Warren fears someone talked. The ba—Orville has disappeared from Helena. Mrs. Jameson claims she saw him in town late last week, but we know the woman's penchant for lying." Mrs. Jameson was Helen's mother, and she was a bitter, angry woman with no regard for the MacKinnons or their friends.

Charlotte's breath left her in a *whoosh*. "He could be on his way here. He could find me." She gazed blankly at the tabletop.

"Boss swears all his men, even the drifters, are loyal," Dixon said. "There is talk that perhaps you *want* to be found. That *you* were the one who wrote him."

Charlotte gasped, wrenching her hands free of Dalton's. She struck, slapping Dixon across the face, before jumping to her feet and backing away from the table. "Get out." When the man gaped at her as though she were deranged, she screamed, "Get out! You have no right to doubt. You have no right to … to …" Tears gushed down her cheeks as her chest heaved. "I trusted you because you worked with Dalton. But you're horrible."

Dalton rose, motioning for Dixon to leave the kitchen.

"No, Dalt. How come she was walkin' in today from the range, all disheveled, with her hair comin' undone?" Dixon asked.

Charlotte shook her head, paling as she saw Dalton freeze in his approach to soothe her. "You'd doubt?" she whispered. She held a quivering hand to rub at her temple. "How could you?"

"Lottie?" Dalton murmured. "What were you doin' on the range?"

"You think I'd meet him?" she whispered, barely able to speak such vile words. "Truly?"

"Tell me."

She stared into her husband's eyes, hating the doubt and fear she saw within. With a long sigh, she said, "For the last several days, I've gone on walks when you ride out. I saw a

174

horse. A beautiful horse. And I finally earned its trust enough to pat it. He's a little skittish, and, when I patted him today, he tossed his head and knocked me down." She shrugged.

"What's he look like?" Dalton asked in a low voice.

"Majestic. Huge. Chestnut-colored."

"You've been tryin' to tame Brutus?" Dixon asked, as though she were the most feeble-minded person he'd ever encountered.

"I don't know who Brutus is, but it's certainly not this horse. He should be called Regal or some other fine name." When her husband snorted and shook his head, she glared at him. She swiped at her cheeks, stepping backward when Dalton moved toward her. "No," she said. "No. You doubted. You are not forgiven." She pushed past him, racing away until the door slammed to the room they shared.

"Dammit," Dalton hissed. "I could have handled that better."

Dixon sighed. "Sorry, Dalt. I made it worse. I filled your head with nonsense."

Dalton sat with a *thunk* at the table again, resting his head in his hands. "I tell her that I trust her, and, at the first sign of trouble, I doubt her. What a fool." He looked at the younger man, who had never claimed to be proficient at love or relationships.

"Boss wants you to come home to the ranch. Doesn't want you out here alone."

Dalton stared at the younger man for a long, hard moment. "Did you come out here to stir up trouble, Dix?"

Dixon's eyes widened, and he shook his head over and over again. "No, Dalt. Of course not. You know what I was like when I arrived at the ranch. I'd never betray you or anyone in our family."

Dalton sighed and pinched the bridge of his nose. He closed his eyes, as his shoulders stooped. "I forgot these hard moments in a marriage," he murmured. "After someone dies, you tend to remember the good times. The laughs. The affection. The joy in her presence." He paused. "You don't dwell on those moments of discord. Or when you acted like an ass and had to apologize."

Dixon took a slurp of water from his glass. "Is it worth it?" he asked. "Seems like you, Boss, and Slims spend an awful lot of time tied up in knots over your women. Maybe it's just better bein' alone."

Dalton laughed and shook his head. "Hell no, it ain't better bein' alone, Dix. I'd take every fight, every moment like this, for one second where I get to hold her. To hear her laugh. Or sing."

Dixon rose and clapped the older man on his shoulder. "Well, I'd get good at grovelin' then, for Miss Charlotte was sure fired up." He nodded to the older man and left to spend the night in the barn.

Sitting alone in the kitchen, Dalton listened as evening settled over the house. Although a small farmhouse, it was comfortable enough, and he wished he and Charlotte would go back to a home like this when they returned to the main ranch. He dreaded living in the home he'd shared with Mary and intermingling his old memories with new ones he now created with Charlotte.

With a groan, he rose, taking a moment to stretch out his muscles, before he moved to their room. At the closed door, he tapped on it softly. When no response came from his knock, he pushed it open. "Lottie?" he whispered. "Love?"

"Don't call me that." She laid curled on her side, a blanket wrapped around her. Her sobs had ceased, and she stared at him with a dull pain in her gaze. "If I were your love, you'd never doubt me."

He approached the bed and dropped to his knees, so he was at her eye level. "That's not true," he said in a low voice.

"I'm human. I'm a man, Charlotte." He sighed as he bowed his head and ran his index finger over his temple. "I have no excuse but to say I froze at the thought of you, out in the fields, completely vulnerable. All I could see was him coming for you, and I would have been nowhere nearby to protect you."

"Don't lie," she said in a scratchy voice. "You paused because you thought I was having secret meetings with him. That I wanted to see him again." She shook her head, as she pushed up, her anger overpowering her sorrow. "How could you?"

"How could I not?" he roared. "How am I to know if you found greater pleasure with him than with me?" He flushed and rose, spinning to face away from her. He slammed his hand against the bedroom door, his breaths emerging as harsh pants.

"What?" she gasped. "What are you talking about?" She slipped from the bed on silent feet, her hands tracing his back. Even though he stiffened at her touch, she continued to softly caress his rigid muscles.

"How do I know you're not dreaming of him, wishing he were by your side rather than some cowpoke with a body that's breakin' down too fast?" he asked with his bowed head. "I know I didn't please you on our weddin' night, Lottie. I know I shouldn't have touched you. I'm sorry." His voice rang with a deep regret.

"Hush," she whispered. "That's not true." She kissed one shoulder and then the other. "You know how much I've loved every moment we spend together. How I wish we had more time for just the two of us."

He shook his head. "No, I don't know. You've never said." He gave an *oof* of surprise when she wrapped her arms around his middle, pressing all along his back.

"You need the words as much as I do," she breathed in

total amazement. "I never realized. ... I never knew." She took a shaky breath. "Every morning I wake alone in our bed, and I wish you were beside me. I ache to feel your arms around me, to hear your husky voice as you whisper to me while you fight sleep, to feel your fingers stroke through my hair."

He turned to meet her earnest, embarrassed gaze. "You speak the truth?"

"Yes," she breathed. "I ... I'm so sorry I ever made you doubt our wedding night. I was overwhelmed. I never knew I could feel so much. So much passion and pleasure. I'd never felt that before." She ducked her head. "I feared you wanted Mary. I didn't know what to do!" she cried out.

"Lottie," he whispered. "You were my dream come to life." His fingers caressed the hair at her temple. "I only thought of you. I promise." He cupped her cheeks, before leaning forward to kiss her softly. "I've been tormented with the belief you dreamed of another."

"Never, Dalton. Never," Charlotte whispered. Taking a deep breath, she whispered, "I realize now, I was never important to him. I could have been anyone to him. You showed me what lovemaking could be like. Should be like."

When he stared at her for a long moment, with a gaze filled with uncertainty, she arched up to kiss him. "Please don't doubt, Dalton. Your faith in me—in us—has been the greatest gift I've ever received." She paled when he shook his head.

"No, Lottie, that's one of my gifts to you." He silenced her with a kiss. "My greatest gift has been, and always will be, my love. I love you, as I never knew I could love." He paused a moment. "I mean no disrespect to Mary, for I loved her too. But what I feel for you is so vibrant. So soul fulfilling." He shrugged, as though he didn't have the words to express what was deep in his heart.

"You love me?" she whispered, her mouth dropped open in shock.

Chuckling, he murmured, "Now who doubts?" as he bent to kiss her parted lips. "Of course I do, my Lottie. My beautiful, giving, passionate, caring wife." He stroked a finger down her delicate jawline. "When a man feels like this, he's not always rational. I'm not," he admitted.

"Do you trust me?" she asked. "Do you believe I'll never betray you?"

"Yes," he said. "I've wondered, for days, about what you do while I'm away. You've been evasive with your answers, when I ask about how you've spent the time I'm away from the ranch."

Pressing forward, Charlotte tucked her head under his jaw. "Oh, Dalton, I wanted to surprise Frederick! I wanted to do something to thank him and to repay him for taking me in when he didn't have to. For giving me a home. I thought I could train this beautiful horse and gift him to Frederick. He'd be a fine stallion for him."

Dalton burst out laughing, his hands running over her head, before cupping her cheeks. "Oh, my precious darlin', do you have no idea who Brutus is? What he did?" When she shook her head in absolute confusion, he said, "Frederick bought him as a gift for his grandfather, Harold. But Brutus was just that, a brute. Couldn't be trained, not even by Bears, the best horse trainer I've ever met. Harold was on the verge of sendin' him east to be made into glue, after Brutus ate one too many pairs of his pantaloons, but thankfully he was in his stall January, a year and a half ago."

"Why?"

"Helen's brother, Walter, was a menace, and his target was Fidelia. Bears's wife." He paused until he saw that she'd made the connection to everyone he mentioned. "Walter followed Fidelia into the livery when it was empty, and somehow Brutus trampled Walter to death, savin' Fidelia."

"Oh my," Charlotte breathed.

"Bears and Fidelia set Brutus free out here as a thank-you to him. And because they knew he was never meant to be tamed." He ran a finger over her cheek again. "Promise me that you won't approach him again. The thought of what he could have done to you these past days will prevent me from sleepin' for a year."

She pressed into his embrace, holding him close. "It's hard to reconcile your story with the horse I've come to know." She sighed. "Not that I know that much about him or horses."

"Promise me, Lottie."

"I promise. I'll remain close to the homestead." She bit her lip as she peered up at him through her lashes. "Will you remain closer too?"

"I only have a few more days' worth of work, and then we should return to the ranch. Boss wants us there so you'll be better protected." He frowned when he saw disappointment in her gaze. "Love?"

"I … I wish our time here had been different," she whispered.

"Different?" he asked. "How?" When she wriggled away, as though she didn't want to speak further on the subject, he held her close. "No, Lottie, you began this conversation. Now you must finish it. Don't be shy. Not with me."

Blushing crimson red, she blurted out, "I hate what Davina and Sorcha will think!" When he stared at her in absolute confusion, she said, "They teased that I'd have weeks and weeks for our honeymoon. Instead all I'll be able to talk about is you working long hours digging post holes and falling asleep over your supper each night out of exhaustion."

"You wanted a honeymoon?" he asked with a shy smile. At her bashful nod and shrug, he let out a loud *whoop*, picking her up and carrying her to their bed. He settled her gently onto the mattress and rested beside her. "Then we'll have a honeymoon," he whispered in her ear. "Digging a post hole could never be as enticing as you, love."

She giggled, wrapping her arms around his neck to pull him close for a kiss.

≈

Charlotte rested on his chest, her fingers playing across his smooth skin. She marveled that his muscles jumped at her soft caress, and she kissed him softly. One of his arms was tangled in her riotous hair, the other looped low over her hips. Their legs remained intertwined, and she sighed as she pushed back.

"No," he gasped. "Please don't leave me." He groaned as though he'd been physically harmed, dropping his arms away. "I'm sorry. If this is what you need ..." He broke off, his eyes closed, and his jaw clenched.

She gazed up at him, her expression softening to one of absolute tenderness, as she saw him attempting to give her what he thought she wanted, even though it went against his deepest desires. "Dalton, my love," she breathed. She waited, but he didn't open his eyes. She traced her fingers over his face, trailing through his stubble until she cupped his jaw. Dissatisfied, she arched up, kissing his jaw before nipping it.

His eyes flew open, and his arms tightened around her again. "Lottie?"

"I ... I feared I was proving myself to be a harlot by wanting to be in your arms. That I should feel ashamed because I relished in every touch, every caress, when I'd so recently thought I loved another." She ducked her head in shame.

"Who fed you such lies?" he rasped. "Adella?" Rolling

Lottie gently to her side, he sheltered her with his large body, cradling her cheeks in his hands.

She nodded, her eyes filled with despair. "I thought I should sleep apart. That it proved I was strong. And that you married a worthy woman." She gasped and clung to his shoulders when he swooped forward to kiss her.

"You are passionate and brave and everything I ever dreamed of and never thought I'd find again." He rested his forehead against hers. "Never doubt how proud I am to call you my wife."

"But, when I tried to seduce you, you stormed away!" she cried, tears leaking onto her cheeks.

He leaned away, staring at her dumfounded. "Seduce me?" He flushed.

"I'd never tease you, Dalton. But I don't know how to be a seductress. I'm a simple woman, and I have no experience with men." She flushed beet red, her gaze dropping to focus on his throat, rather than the incredulous look in his gaze. "I don't even know if you like what we did. Now or on our honeymoon."

He gave an incredulous snort of laughter. "You'd doubt?" At the wounded look in her gaze, he kissed her nose and cheeks as he murmured, "Oh, love, Slims is right. We must talk. Everything is worse with silence." He stared deeply into her beautiful eyes.

"Do you wish you had Mary in your arms rather than me?"

"Oh, dear God, no," he breathed, rolling them again so she rested against his chest. He wrapped his arms and legs around her as though his full body hug could alleviate all her doubts and fears. "Never. I rejoice in every moment I have you in my arms. Every moment you trust me to give you pleasure. And I pray I do please you."

She frowned, as she wriggled against him to free an arm,

so she could run a hand through his disheveled hair. "Why would you doubt?" she whispered, gazing into his eyes, as though mesmerized by what she saw.

"Do you remember when I approached you with the preacher? You said to me, 'That what I thought was true was a lie.'" He paused, as he gathered his thoughts. "What if the truth that was a lie was your feelings for me?"

"No, Dalton, no," she said in a rush. "You have to understand. I was talking about Adella and the tea. I was so confused. Please."

His eyes shone with love as he gazed at her. "Understand this, Lottie. I was filled with fear. What if you dreamed of him? Wished you were with him?" Her sweet smile caused his breath to catch.

"Never," she vowed. "He will only be a memory I wish to forget. Every touch, every kiss from you helps me forget him a little more." She leaned forward, her lips hovering over his. "Help me leave him behind, Dalton."

He groaned, kissing her softly. As he deepened the kiss, he broke away for a moment to murmur, "With the greatest pleasure, my love."

The following morning, Dalton rose late, unwilling to leave his wife's company. However, he knew he needed to speak with Dixon, before he departed. Stepping onto the front porch with a cup of day-old cold coffee, he saw Dixon, repairing the chicken coop. "Why are you doing that, Dix?"

Dixon turned to shrug. "Seemed better than doin' nothin'. If I'd known I'd be here waiting for a man who's wooin' his wife, I would have brought one of my novels with me. The roof needs work, but it shouldn't take much time to get it functional again." He turned his focus from the chicken coop to study his friend. "Is everything all right with your missus?"

Unable to suppress a satisfied grin, Dalton nodded. "Aye," he murmured. "Everything's better than all right." He shifted his feet. "Would you tell Boss we won't be returnin' right away? We want a little while longer out here, before we have to return."

Dixon grinned. "Sure. I know Boss envies you. He'd like a little time away with Miss Sorcha, but he won't have that now that they have the twins." He shrugged. "I doubt Boss really minds."

"No," Dalton said, the memory of holding little Harold flashing through his mind. "I doubt he does."

"Sorry I stirred up trouble last night," Dixon said.

Dalton threw the day-old coffee that tasted like sludge into the dirt. "I'm not. You helped us, Dix. Thanks."

The younger man shrugged, moving into the barn to saddle up his horse and to head back to the main ranch. Dalton waved at Dixon when he rode out, ignoring the work that he should do that day. Rather than rush to saddle his horse and ride out onto the rangeland to dig more post holes, he turned back toward the farmhouse. Toward his wife.

Poking his head into the kitchen, he saw the stove was still banked, and no fresh coffee had been started. Deciding that the few swigs of the day-old brew would suffice, he kicked off his boots and reentered their bedroom, halting at the sight of Charlotte curled up on the bed. Her hair was an unruly mess, shining like a red and gold kaleidoscope in the sun's rays. Her lips were turned up in a soft smile.

Stripping his clothes, he slipped back into bed, wrapping his arms around her. He kissed her head and then her shoulder, his fingers playing over the satiny skin of her back. He was unable to keep himself from touching her.

"Where did you go?" she murmured in a sleep-slurred

voice. Her fingers reached up, caressing his face, her fingers scraping over his stubble.

"I dreamed of this," he rasped. "Of you wanting to be in my arms. Of breathing in the intoxicating scent of your hair and feeling it tickle my nose and slide across my chest. Of you running your hands over my cheeks." His eyes glowed with a deep emotion. "I feared it would forever remain a dream."

"Dalton," she breathed, her eyes filled with adoration. "Forgive me for all the time we lost. Forgive me …" She gasped as he kissed her.

"No," he rasped, as he rocked her side to side. "There's nothing to forgive. We needed time to arrive at this moment. We needed time to realize what we have is precious." Her luminous smile made his breath hitch.

"*Precious*," she said, as she pushed up to brush her lips over his. "To be cherished. And well tended."

He groaned, rolling her over. "God, how I love you, Lottie."

"Show me," she said with a passionate sigh, as he kissed her neck. "And let me show you, too."

CHAPTER 14

A week later, Frederick had come and gone. After being reassured that all was well and that both Charlotte and Dalton desired more time on the distant homestead without further interference, Frederick had sent out supplies that could last them two more weeks. Frederick had appeared apologetic when he informed Dalton that he was needed back at the main ranch at the end of the two weeks. Dalton had slapped Boss on his back, thankful for the generous time with his wife, away from the busy ranch.

Charlotte covered the loaves of bread she set into the bread pans to rise, swiping at her perspiring forehead. She had hoped the day would prove cooler than the previous three days. However, they were out of bread, and she felt she had no choice but to bake bread, even in the sweltering heat.

She grabbed her knitting needles, determined to knit a blue scarf to match Dalton's eyes, and settled on the porch in the rocker, hoping for a breeze. Sorcha had sent new yarn in the supplies Frederick had shipped out to them, as though understanding Charlotte would need more than cooking to fill her time while Dalton worked on the homestead. Sorcha had also added the most recent newspaper, and Charlotte flushed as she recalled all that Jessamine had written in her *Fact or Fiction* section.

FACT OR FICTION

Imagine my surprise to hear a most fascinating tale, as I sat on my newspaper office stoop, suffering in this stifling heat. One of our estimable townsfolk, who will remain anonymous, relayed to me that one of our newest citizens has claim to a great deal more notoriety than she cared to impart.

Now, dear reader, I am still uncertain of the veracity of this tale. I fear the title of this column would more appropriately be titled Farce or Fantasy. *However, this fine gentleman swore on a Bible that his tale was as good as the gospel. If he is to be believed, the woman who recently married the esteemed ranch hand, Mr. Dalton, is, in fact, the wayward daughter of a Mr. Harland Jackman.*

Now I can hear you saying to yourself, Why should I care who Mr. Harland Jackman is? *If you recall, he was a preeminent explorer, who documented the natural world before we attempted to tame it. His writing and paintings have helped those mired in the cities to imagine what the wilds of our world are like. In fact, his sketches of native plants and trees were recently posthumously published to great acclaim in New York City.*

When I inquired about the use of the last name, Ingram, *it appears Charlotte has used her mother's name from infancy, as her father died soon after her birth, in a brutal bear attack. In a desire to prevent unwanted interest in Mr. Jackman's only living child, her mother attempted to shield her from intrusive inquiries. Rather than return to their lavish homes in the outskirts of our nation's capital, her mother and grandmother fulfilled his wishes and remained in a remote part of Montana, raising Charlotte alone,*

with no knowledge of her famous father, intent on sheltering her
from the spurious claims to her fortune.

Now, I ask you, dear reader. Is this Fact or Fiction?

Charlotte made a sound of disgust as she reread Jessamine's article. "Hogwash, all of it." She laughed, setting aside the paper. "At least she's made me seem more intriguing than I truly am. And the paper will make good kindling."

Humming to herself, rocking, her knitting lay dormant in her lap as her mind replayed scenes from the previous evenings. Always they were filled with conversation, laughter, and passion. She sighed with happiness that Dalton never used the pain of her past against her, instead focusing on the future and the new memories he hoped to create. He had taken her at her word, intent on replacing every memory she had of Orville with better and more passionate moments with Dalton.

"Soon Orville will be nothing more than a distant memory," she said to herself.

She heard the sound of a twig snapping nearby and looked up. Listening intently, she hoped to see Dalton striding from the barn. However, she knew it was barely past midday. He took his responsibilities to Frederick seriously, and she'd never wish for him to sacrifice his standards for her. With a sigh, she hummed again and rocked in the chair in the shade, praying for a breeze.

At the sound of another twig breaking, she glanced up. Dropping her knitting needles, she rose to race into the house. At the shattering of the wood on the doorjamb directly to her right, the sound of a gunshot ricocheted around her, and she froze.

"You can't escape me, Charlotte," Orville Coldwell said with a sneering laugh. "I've had to bide my time. But I've found my way to you." He was tall, almost as tall as Warren, and he appeared urbane, even though he didn't wear a suit. His boots were new, their polish dusty. His cambric shirt starched, as though awaiting a collar and a waistcoat. He didn't wear the typical cowboy hat but instead wore a hat with a flatter brim. Although it appeared he attempted to blend in, as though he were any other cowboy, he was as out of place as a buffalo in a sitting room.

"Why?" she gasped. "I'm a married woman. You shouldn't want anything to do with me."

Orville waved the gun around, indicating she was to step away from the house. He nodded as she took jerky steps toward the side of the house and in the direction of the rangeland. "Oh, I want to know something. Did you enjoy ridiculing Adella? Making yourself feel superior because you can have a child, and she's barren?"

Shaking her head, Charlotte stumbled as she walked backward. She was intent on watching the gun he waved around like a lunatic, although she wasn't certain why. She could do nothing to stop a bullet from ripping apart her vulnerable flesh. "No. I'd never do that to another woman."

"You soulless hussy!" he screeched. "You already have. You denied us the child we should have had. All you had to do was agree to give us what was rightfully mine. My child."

Charlotte shook her head. "No. You had no right to ask. To demand. And no right to have me beaten and left for dead." She continued to stumble backward, praying for Dalton to return home early. To save her from being forced to wander any farther away from the homestead, a place that had become her sanctuary, with the man of her nightmares.

"Of course I wanted you dead," Orville snapped. "If you wouldn't give us the baby and make us parents, then what good were you?"

Charlotte shook her head, over and over, as she backed away from him. "Did you ever like me at all?"

He snorted and rolled his eyes. "*Like* had nothing to do with it. You were an easy target. You had no one to protect you, and you were with little sense. Your knowledge of men was abysmal, and your flirting skills were worse than a seven-year-old's."

She flushed at his criticism. "My husband doesn't complain."

"A man who spends his time living in the remote back-country of Montana will be thankful for any woman willing to warm his bed." He gazed at her pityingly. "Adella mentioned your delusions that the man truly cared for you."

"Of course Dalton cares," Charlotte said, her gaze roving wildly for anything she could use as a weapon. "You should leave now before he finds you here."

Orville took a lunging step toward her. Charlotte shrieked, jerking backward and almost losing her balance. She regained her footing, barely scooting out of his grasp. She felt the air move where his hands swatted in their attempt to grab her.

He smiled with a maniacal joy. "I love our cat-and-mouse game. It reminds me of when I was convincing you to trust me. To let me into your bed. It's a pity you played the upstanding virgin for so long. We could have had more time together before I had to leave town."

Charlotte shook, battling her memories of her time with him. "And I can only wish I'd had even less time to spend in your arms."

"Oh, come. Your protestations ring hollow. I doubt you'll ever have another lover like me."

She nodded. "You're right. I'll never again allow a selfish brute, intent only on his own pleasure, in my bed ever again." She shrieked again as his arm lunged forward, smacking her in her cheek. She careened backward, landing on her back.

Her legs tangled in her skirts, but she scrambled up just as he approached her.

"Why rise when I know you prefer to have our rendezvous laying down?" he sneered, gripping her arms.

"Let me go!" she yelled, kicking at his legs and attempting to stomp on his feet. Her efforts earned her a few grunts but did not grant her freedom.

"Come. I've had enough chatter. I'm taking you away from here. I'm certain your husband will believe you'd prefer my company to his." He jerked on her arm, propelling her away from the homestead.

"No," she cried. "I promised I wouldn't leave." She stumbled, falling to her knees. However, Orville showed her no solicitude, jerking her upright to propel her farther and farther away. When she walked over a rise and saw a horse tied to a tree, she dug in her heels. "No," she gasped again. "It's not safe. That horse isn't tamed."

"I've had enough!" he shrieked. "You will get on that horse, and you will cease fighting me. Imagine my surprise when I realized you were a secret heiress."

"A secret heiress?" Charlotte asked. "Are you delusional?"

"I read the article, just like everyone else in town. I was the only one astute enough to act. You're coming with me to Butte. You're signing over your father's legacy to me."

Charlotte shook her head in disbelief. "I have no legacy. You don't understand." She shrieked as he waved the gun in front of her face, nearly hitting her in the head.

"No, *you* don't understand. I will have your money. Not your worthless husband. Now get on the horse!" Orville ignored Brutus flapping his ears and tossing his head, as he pawed the ground with agitation. With a grunt, Orville threw her on the stallion's back. He moved to untie Brutus from the tree, screaming in agony as Brutus yanked on the reins, freeing himself.

Brutus reared, causing Orville to cower. Standing on his haunches, Brutus punched wildly with his front hooves, until one of them pummeled Orville's right arm and shoulder. With a snort, Brutus landed down on all fours with a thunderous *clomp*, narrowly missing trampling Orville. Brutus pivoted away, racing over the prairie, with Charlotte clutching at his mane.

Her teeth rattling, her back jarring, and her legs gripping Brutus's flanks, Charlotte held on for dear life. She knew if she let go, she would suffer a severe body blow and would be knocked unconscious in the middle of nowhere. Praying for calm, she murmured to the stallion, "Regal, please, there's no danger now. We're fine. I'm fine. You left the bad man behind. Please, Regal. Don't hurt me." She pressed her tearstained face to Brutus's neck, quivering with relief as the punishing gallop slowed to a trot and then a walk.

She continued to cling to the stallion, completely disoriented and terrified. If she focused hard, she knew she might discern where she was. However, after the shock of seeing Orville and the flight across the rangeland on Brutus, she decided to trust in the horse's instincts.

As her arms and legs went numb from clutching Brutus, she feared she would involuntarily fall off his back. "Please, please, let us arrive to wherever we are going soon," she pleaded. She kept her head down, unwilling to face the reality she could be traveling farther into the wilderness. Farther away from Dalton.

Her mind imagined how her husband would feel when he arrived home to find her missing. Would he understand she did not leave of her own volition? Or would he imagine the worst? She hoped the previous days they'd had together would give him the confidence to know she would never willingly return to a man like Orville.

She heard what sounded like a man's voice and then a

whistle. Her head jerked up, and she moaned from the stiff-ness of being in the same position for so long. She saw Slims, Frederick, Shorty, and Dixon approaching her on horseback, and fresh tears coursed down her cheeks. However, as they neared Brutus, the feral horse whinnied and raced in the opposite direction.

"No, please, no," she gasped. "Help me!" she screamed.

After a few more bone-jarring strides, Brutus stopped his mad dash, snorted and stomped his feet, but remained in one place.

"There's a good boy," she soothed, as she tried to ease her stranglehold on his mane. Her cramped fingers finally let go, and she gasped with pain as she moved her arms. She slid around so both legs were to one side and hoped the drop to the ground wasn't too far. With a small prayer, she let go, falling the few feet before she landed with another bone-jarring *thud*. "Ouch!" she cried out.

The moment she was off his back, Brutus reared up and whinnied. He then took off, racing a short distance away, before he pranced around to face her. She remained on the ground, unable to move.

"Charlotte!" Frederick screamed, as he raced toward her. His horse kicked up dirt near her, as he vaulted off Boots. Kneeling beside her, Frederick reached out a hand, stilling his frantic movements when she flinched. "Charlotte," he said in a low voice, his blue eyes gleaming with terror. "You're well. You're safe. Let Slims help you to the ranch. We'll care for you."

"Dalton," she whispered. "He'll hurt Dalton."

"Damnation," Shorty muttered, spinning his horse away from them, as he raced across the grange land, Dixon following him.

"Short will marshal men to ride to the new homestead. Nothing will happen to Dalton," Frederick said in a soothing voice. "Come. Let's get you home, so Sorcha and Davina can spoil you." He hefted her up, handing her to Slims.

Charlotte shook the entire ride back, thankful they rode at a slow pace. Thankful for Slims's strong arms around her. She was unable to hold on after her desperate ride on Brutus's back.

Davina stood on the front porch, her hand over her eyes, as she acted as sentry. "Charlotte!" she cried out, when she ran down the drive to meet them. "Slims, tell me she's all right. She's no' hurt, aye?"

Slims motioned for her to back up, as he handed Charlotte down to Frederick. "I can't make promises. She's shakin' worse than a leaf before a fall storm, and she won't talk. I think she's in shock."

Sorcha raced from the house, her red-brown hair a tangle down her back. "Charlotte!" she cried out. "What did the man do to ye?"

At the quiet words and the soft hands of Sorcha and Davina, Charlotte felt her overwhelming numbness evaporate. Deep sobs erupted, and she shook her head, unable to speak.

"Give her space, love," Frederick said. "Let's get her comfortable. And then we must wait for Dalton to arrive."

"Dalton," Charlotte gasped. "Please, let him be safe."

Dalton rode back to the Henderson farmhouse in the late afternoon. He knew during these long summer days that he should work until the early evening. However, the lure of spending more time with Charlotte was too great to ignore. Especially now that she desired time with him. Now that she ached for his kisses, as he did hers, he found he could not resist her. Smiling like a lovesick fool, he whistled as he neared the barn. *This is what was meant by a honeymoon*, he thought. He gave thanks they hadn't squandered all of their time alone.

Although Frederick had sent out food for another two weeks, they were almost through those supplies. He knew they would need to return to the main ranch soon. Unable to fight the regret of leaving this small home, he wished he had such a space to return to. Nothing so big as this house, but a new home that would be just for the two of them and their new memories. He knew now that he could never fully ignore the memories of Mary dying in the cabin that sat empty. He did not need to hear the silent echoes of her agonizing screams. He wanted a fresh start. With a sigh, he understood he should be thankful he would have anything more than the tiny room in the bunkhouse for them.

As his horse clopped into the drive, he frowned with disappointment. The previous days, Charlotte had been on the front porch, eagerly awaiting his arrival. Today she was nowhere to be found. He moved into the barn, tended to his horse, and walked toward the house. "Charlotte?" he called out. "Lottie?"

The sound of a *click* echoed in the silent afternoon, and he stilled. Unless he was wrong, someone had just cocked a pistol. He scanned in front of him and didn't see a threat. With slow, measured movements, he spun around, coming to a halt to find a man now seated on an overturned crate with a pistol held awkwardly in his left hand.

Dalton held his hands up, having no desire to be shot so far from help. "My guess is that you're Orville Coldwell."

The man sweated profusely, even though he sat in the building's shade, his brown hair plastered to his head, as a small rivulet of sweat raced down one cheek. "Aren't you the clever one?" he said in a mocking tone.

That voice only distantly reminded Dalton of Warren

Clark. This man retained much more of the upper-class accent than Warren had, and Orville looked uncomfortable without a waistcoat and a tie. Although he wore clothes that should have made him look like a hired hand, he was too refined to ever pass for cowboy. "What have you done to Lottie?"

He sneered at Dalton. "Who's to say I've done anything to her? You should know how your wife is, always eager for a little attention."

Dalton's muscles tightened, but he attempted to appear relaxed in front of the man's taunts. "Lottie!" he screamed. "Yell and tell me that you're all right."

Orville chuckled. "You are a fool to worry about such an inferior woman." The hand pointing the gun at Dalton tapped forward as though emphasizing his point. "I know my Adella informed you of the same. She warned you not to marry her."

"Why should I take advice from a woman who only wanted to use Charlotte as a broodmare?" Dalton continued to listen for any sign of his wife, as he inched toward the side of the house.

Laughing, Orville rocked backward, gasping in pain at the movement. "Damnation," he swore, as fresh sweat bloomed on his forehead. "You should know that's all women are good for. Except mine. Can't even give me a child."

Ignoring his talk about children, Dalton frowned, noticing that Orville's right arm hung uselessly by his side. "Seems you had yourself an accident."

"I don't need to have a conversation with you about a rogue horse," Orville snapped, waving the gun around wildly.

"Rogue horse," Dalton whispered, his mind racing at the implications. "*Brutus.*"

"*Brutal* is more like it," Orville said.

Dalton leaped to the side, landing on his stomach, as a

shot flew wide. He jumped up and ran to the side of the house, listening intently as the man moaned about his arm. Walking with stealthy intent, Dalton circled the small house, picking up a large branch of wood. As he rounded the final wall, he saw Orville hunched forward, muttering to himself. If he approached the man, Dalton would be completely exposed.

Indecision filled him, as he had no desire to be shot. However, he feared Charlotte was injured somewhere on the open prairie, and he had no idea how he would find her. He fought terror at the thought of her being anywhere near Brutus, but he feared she might have been.

He heard a distant whistle and looked to the drive to see six men galloping toward the homestead. He waved his branch, hoping to earn their attention, but knew they couldn't see him behind the house. "Men are coming, Orville. If you shoot at one of them, you're dead. Put the gun down."

Orville looked over his shoulder, pointed the gun, and shot in his direction. Dalton ducked backward, swearing as the bullet ricocheted off the side of the house and nearly nicked him.

"Idiot!" Dalton yelled. However, the gun firing had warned the approaching men. He looked around the house again, swearing, as he no longer saw Orville. Slipping around the side of the house, he inched his way toward the front of the house again. When he reached the front corner, he peered around the side, but Orville was nowhere in sight.

Just then the men thundered in on horseback, pistols and rifles cocked. Dalton held up his hands. "Don't shoot!" he called out.

Shorty jumped down and raced to him. "What's goin' on, Dalt?"

"That bastard Orville's around here somewhere. Warren's cousin. Shootin' like a crazy man with his left hand. Hurt his right arm. Don't know where he went." His gaze was wild. "I don't know where Lottie is. What he's done to her. I fear she's out on the range, injured and alone."

Shorty made a soothing noise as he watched other hands dismount and fan out to search the homestead. "Your wife's back at the big house, and she's traumatized after her ride across the prairie on Brutus's back." Shaking his head at Dalton, who wanted to ask him more questions, he said, "You can find out when you arrive. She was in shock but appeared otherwise well, when I left. For now, get your horse, and we'll head home."

Dalton paused to stare at three of the hands, who had walked into the small farmhouse, searching for Orville. They came out with a shake of their heads. "Just some bread rising in the kitchen," one of them said.

Suddenly the barn door burst open, and Orville galloped out on Dalton's horse, racing down the drive.

"He's stealin' my horse!" Dalton yelled, taking a step forward, but knowing he could do nothing.

"Like hell he is," Dixon said, rising up in his saddle and taking aim with his rifle. He shot once and gave a satisfied nod.

They watched as Orville fell to the side, off the horse, crumpling to the ground.

"Did you kill him?" Dalton asked, as he gaped at the younger man in wonder.

"I doubt it," Dixon said. "I aimed for his shoulder. Figured it was already so messed up that a bullet wouldn't hurt it that much worse."

Shorty chuckled. "I doubt he'll agree with your logic." He watched as Dalton's horse trotted into the yard. "Come on. Let's get goin'. I'd imagine Miss Charlotte is gettin' anxious to see her husband."

Dalton worked on his saddle, cinching the fastenings,

before mounting to ride out with his friends. They trotted out of the yard, pausing where Orville had fallen on the drive. One of the men hopped down and pick up Orville's gun. Another hoisted him onto the back of an unsaddled horse he'd brought from the barn, belly down, tying him in place.

Dalton leaned over to gaze into Orville's pain glazed, hate filled gaze. "There. Now you'll have an idea of what my wife suffered." He rose, urging his horse into a gallop as he raced toward Charlotte.

CHAPTER 15

Dalton burst into the big house, ignoring every mandate of keeping a moderated voice and to never make noise for fear of waking the twins. *Let them howl,* he thought as he bellowed, "Charlotte!" His boots clomped to a halt as he looked around, uncertain where to go. He wanted to see his wife and to see her now, but he felt awkward roaming through Boss's home.

"Dalton," Sorcha called out, her head poking out of the downstairs bedroom that had been used as a sickroom in the past. "Come."

Dalton raced to her, barreling into the room. He fell to his knees at the sight of Charlotte unconscious on the bed, her chest slowly rising and falling in an even cadence. "Lottie." He looked at Charlotte, his eyes rounded with horror. "Is she … is she dying?"

"Nae," Sorcha said, as she ran a hand down his arm. "She's exhausted. Sleepin' deeply. Sit by her, an' be here when she wakes. She'll recover, Dalton." She slipped from the room, shutting the door behind her.

Dalton collapsed onto the chair by Charlotte's side, his

head bowed, as a litany of jumbled-up words filled his mind. The one coherent thought was *Please, recover. Please, come back to me*. Over and over again, he said those words to himself. He kissed her hand, holding it to his lips, as tears silently fell, and he rocked forward and back.

Finally he rose, kicked off his boots and socks, and gingerly crawled over her. "I need to hold you, my Lottie," he whispered. "Sitting on a chair just isn't close enough, my love." He kissed her head as he eased it up, so he could slip his arm underneath and could settle her on his shoulder. "There, where you're supposed to be. Snuggled up in my arms." He kissed her head.

Unable to cease talking to her, he rambled on and on. "I knew something was wrong the moment you weren't on the front porch to welcome me. I know it's silly, darlin', but I've come to love that tradition. Having you wait on the front porch for me is something I look forward to. After a hard day's work, seeing you makes it all worthwhile." He sighed as he kissed her head. "I know you'll have other more important things to do with your time than rush to greet me, but you'll never know what it's meant to me that you're as eager to see me as I am to see you."

He ran his hands over her, caressing her, as she continued to sleep against him. He took solace in the constant beat of her heart and the steady rise and fall of her chest. Kissing her head, he willed her to wake. To kiss him back. To speak with him. In the deepest recesses of his heart, he yearned for her to confess her love for him. For he couldn't fathom loving her as he did without her feeling the same.

He sighed, his hold on her easing. "Ah, Lottie love, how did you steal my heart in such a short time?"

"It wasn't short," she murmured.

"Lottie!" he exclaimed, easing his shoulder out from

under her, so she was on the pillow. "Please tell me. What I can do for you?"

"Nothing," she whispered, her eyes opening. "Nothing but continue to hold me. Talk with me. Reassure me that I'm not alone."

"No, darlin', you aren't alone. I promise you. You'll never be alone. I'll muck out stalls every day so you aren't alone."

She huffed out an amused breath, turning her face into his neck. "Don't be foolish," she whispered. "I love how you smell. Of sweat and faded sandalwood and horses. All mine."

He groaned and wrapped his arms around her, pulling her even tighter to him. "Lottie, what happened? Why are you here? What was Orville doing at our ... the homestead?"

She moaned as she pushed away from him. "Oh, dizzy," she breathed, holding a hand to her head as she rested against a pillow. Opening her eyes, she was filled with reassurance as she gazed upon her husband and raised a shaking hand to cup his jaw. "My muscles are worn out from clinging to Brutus. Regal. Whatever he's called."

Dalton clamped his jaw, as he fought an overwhelming sense of impotent panic. "What happened?"

Her hand dropped, resting on his chest. "I was sitting on the front porch. Singing. Dreaming. Thinking about Jessamine's latest article." She flushed. "The past few days, I've wandered to the front porch a bit earlier each day. Hoping you'd return a little earlier." She flushed and ducked her head.

He chuckled, his worries momentarily forgotten. "Good," he murmured, as he ran his fingers through her silky hair. "I worried I was the only one acting like a lovesick calf." His grin faded as he saw the echo of terror in her gaze. "Lottie, my love, what did he do to you?"

Her eyes widened, and she grunted and groaned as she attempted to push herself up. However, her arms were too weak, and she collapsed on his chest with a whimper. "He didn't hurt me. I swear." She relaxed, as his strong arms wrapped around her. "He wanted to take me to Butte. Wanted the money he thought I had inherited from my father."

"What inheritance?"

She smiled at the abject confusion in his gaze. "Jessamine wrote a foolish article about me, where a man claims my father was a famous botanist. That I had riches waiting for me, if only I were to claim them. None of it's true." She sighed. "But Orville thought it was and wanted the money. Somehow he thought he could force me to Butte to sign over my nonexistent inheritance to him."

Dalton shivered. "Don't torment me with what he would have done to you once he realized you couldn't give him what he wanted."

Her eyes widened, as though remembering the beating she'd already suffered at Orville's hands. "Orville thought he had found the perfect horse to aid him."

Dalton shuddered, his hands running over her back, reassuring himself that she was alive and well in his arms. "God, Lottie. You'll give me nightmares until I die. What did Brutus do?"

"Once I'd been thrown up on the stallion's back, he reared, jerking the rope from Orville's hand. Regal kicked at Orville, knocking him to the ground and then raced away." She spoke as though in a trance, as though it had occurred to someone else. "I held on for dear life. I knew if I fell, you'd never find me, that I'd be injured and alone on the rangeland, a prime target for coyotes or wolves." She pressed her head against his chest to banish such imaginings. "Regal ran and ran and ran to the point I thought I couldn't hold on anymore. But I did. I did."

He smiled at the pride in her voice. "Of course you did.

You're brave and strong and capable. Somehow that ornery horse knew to bring you here." His hands clutched her. "I can't bear to imagine what might have happened to you."

She pressed her face to his shoulder, her breath stuttering, as a few tears leaked out. Soon a torrent of emotions poured forth, and he held her as she sobbed. "I'm sorry. I know I'm safe."

Dalton kissed her head again, breathing in her subtle lilac and soap scent. When he left the house this morning, he never would have thought he'd be on the verge of losing what he held most dear in this life. Not so soon again. "I don't know what I would have done had I lost you, Lottie." He ran his hand over her tearstained cheeks, gazing with an impassioned fervency into her eyes. "If you'd been on that prairie, I would have found you. Someway, somehow. I would have found you, my love."

She shivered, speaking in a quivering voice, "I'm thankful you didn't need to." She took a deep breath. "All I could think about, as I bounced along on Regal's—Brutus's—back, was you." She stared, mesmerized, into his eyes. "I knew, if something happened, I would die with the greatest regret." She gasped as his hands tightened at the mention of her dying.

"I can't lose you, Lottie," he whispered.

Her eyes filled, and she stroked a hand over his cheek. "I know. I feel the same about you. The thought Orville might have hurt you. That it would have been my fault." Her mouth quivered. "It was a fear almost past bearing."

Dalton shook his head. "It would have been no one's fault but his. He's the lunatic." After a long moment, he asked, "What would have been your regret?"

Charlotte took a steadying breath. "I love you," she said in a soft but confident voice. "So much. And I worried I'd never have the chance to tell you."

"Lottie," he murmured, pulling her close and burying his head in the wild mass of her hair. "God, how I love you."

"I refused to believe fate would be so cruel to take me away from you before I could tell you."

Running his fingers over her cheeks, he shook his head. "I pray it won't be so cruel as to take you from me now either. I need you, love."

She smiled radiantly. "As I need you." She arched forward, kissing him. She sighed with pleasure, breaking the kiss and relaxing in his arms.

At the knock on the door a moment later, Dalton looked over his shoulder. "Yes?" he called out.

Frederick poked his head in. "I wanted to ensure all was well. We have supper waiting, but we could bring it to you on trays, if you prefer."

Dalton nodded his head at the second option, and Frederick winked before backing out.

"No," Charlotte protested. "They've already done so much. We shouldn't put them to more work."

Smoothing his hands over her, he eased her of any desire to rise from the comfort of his arms. "No, love, let them continue to care for us. We'll thank them in the morning." He sighed with contentment to hold her safe in his arms, as she slipped into sleep once more, thankful to have his friends around him.

Charlotte emerged from the bedroom the next day in time for the midday meal. Rubbing a hand over her growling stomach, she entered the kitchen. "*Oof*," she gasped, as she was enveloped in a hug.

"Don't you ever scare us like that again, young lady. Do you hear me?" Irene said, as she squeezed her tight.

"Mrs. Tompkins," Charlotte stammered. "I … I'm sorry."

"Don't you go apologizin' to her when it ain't your fault some madman put you on the back of my lunatic horse," Harold said, hauling her close for his embrace and a kiss on her head. "We're relieved to see you looking so well."

"What are you doing here?" Charlotte asked, staring with confusion from one to the other, as though they were apparitions. "I thought you had a café to run."

"Oh, the townsfolk'll survive a day or two without us. We had to ensure our Dalton wasn't going to suffer another misfortune. That boy's endured enough. If there was anythin' we could do, we wanted to be here to help."

Nodding, Charlotte edged away from them. "Of course. I'm delighted you're here to reassure yourselves that Dalton is well." She stilled when Irene rested a hand on her forearm.

"You do understand he wouldn't have been well if you'd been harmed?" Irene asked with a frown.

Harold scratched at his head as he studied Charlotte. "Come. Let me tell you a story. Ireney saved you some food, and I can imagine you'd like a cup of coffee." He waved away her protestations. "Dalton's busy with Fred in his office, and he'll be here soon. We have a surprise for the two of you, and we had to keep the boy busy until you woke up."

At the delighted, curious gleam in her eyes, he grinned. "You'll have to wait for him. And he wouldn't want you to be hungry, so eat up." Harold settled in the comfortable chair at the head of the table, while Charlotte sat on a bench by his side. "Now I can imagine what your life was like as a child. Filled with loneliness. A miserable mother or father. No loving siblings." Harold shrugged, as though it were a story he'd heard too often for his liking. "We have a tendency to attract that sort of stray." He grunted when Irene tapped him on his head.

"They aren't strays, Harold," Irene muttered. "They're our family."

Shrugging unrepentantly, Harold grinned at Charlotte, as he sipped at his coffee. "If you had a strong family or ties you couldn't break, you wouldn't be here with us now. That much I know is true." He awaited her protestations, and, when none came, he gave a grunt of self-acknowledgment at his logic. "Now Irene and I met when we were young. Sweethearts."

Irene rolled her eyes, although she couldn't hide the flirting smile of her lips or the sparkle in her gaze when she stared at her husband of over fifty years.

Charlotte giggled around a bite of scrambled eggs.

"Do you know the greatest sadness, Charlotte?" Harold asked. At the shake of her head, he said, "It's to yearn for something with all your soul and to be denied it." He stared at Irene. "Thankfully I've always had my Ireney. But we never had the houseful of children we desired."

"I thought you had a son," Charlotte said.

"Ah, yes, our boy," Harold said. "Headstrong and too proud for his own good. We loved him somethin' fierce. But we learned we couldn't smother him with all the love we had inside us. Rather than drown in regret at not havin' the ten children we desired"—he winked at Irene as she snorted —"we opened our hearts to those who were like family to us. Our hired hands. Our friends in town. And now we have a life fuller than I ever would have thought possible."

Irene sniffled and nodded.

"I don't understand," Charlotte whispered.

"You're precious to us because you're precious to Dalton," Harold said. "But, if you'd allow it, you'd be precious to us simply because of who you are. Let us love you like grand-parents."

Charlotte's fork clattered to the table, and she covered

her gaping mouth with her hand. She shook her head, over and over again in tiny motions, panicked gasps emerging.

Harold's delighted expression faded, as he stared at the sign of her distress. "Charlotte? I'm sorry if the thought of us caring for you is dreadful."

"Not dreadful," she gasped out. "Unexpected. Like a Christmas gift. I … I don't know what your kind of caring means." She swallowed as she stared from Irene to Harold again and again. "I've never had someone offer me—" Her voice broke.

"Love," Irene said in a soft voice. "Yes, you have, child. I know Dalton's offered you his."

Harold reached forward, his gnarled, callused hand swiping her cheeks. "Are you tellin' me no one's ever given you a Christmas gift?" At her flushed bow of her head, he muttered his displeasure.

"I'm afraid I'll disappoint you," Charlotte gasped out. "I … Dalton tells me that I don't have to earn love, but I don't know how to not lose it if I haven't earned it."

Irene made a soothing sound and sat down, forcing Charlotte to scoot down the bench. Irene wrapped an arm around the younger woman's back, encouraging her to lean her head on her sturdy shoulder. "Now you must rid yourself of such nonsense. You don't need to earn anything. You are precious as you are. If you do something that offends or bothers us, we will tell you."

Harold spoke up. "Did Warren lose the family's regard after concealing his cousin's part in your misfortune?" He shook his head. "No. We were upset, but we'd never act so rashly as to hurt him. That's not what family does. That's not who we are."

Charlotte rested her head against Irene's shoulder. "I wasn't raised like this. With understanding and kindness."

Irene chuckled. "Well, if we smother you with it now, let

us know." She looked to the door, her smile broadening at the sight of Dalton, leaning against the doorjamb. "And now I believe it's time for your surprise."

Dalton's eyes glowed with a soft joy at the sight of Irene, the woman who had been like a mother to him for so many years, caring for his wife. He thought his heart would burst at seeing Harold and Irene care so tenderly for Charlotte. "Surprise?" he murmured. "Is it news that Orville died overnight?"

"Oh, hush," Irene ordered. "You don't want such bad tidings so early in your marriage. And you don't want Dixon to have to suffer an inquest. No, the sorry man's in town. Helen sewed him up last night. Did enough bellyachin' to keep most of us awake late into the night."

"Why didn't the doc help?" Dalton asked.

"He was off helping at a mining disaster," Harold said. "Warren insisted on stayin' in town until his useless cousin was shipped out. Should happen sometime this mornin'. He'll be sent back to Butte."

Standing tall with his hands on his hips, Dalton shook his head. "I want there to be some consequences for how he treated Lottie. I don't want anyone thinkin' they can show up and hurt her."

Irene laughed. "Believe me. No one does. Between a dislocated shoulder and a bullet in the same shoulder, none will bother you again, Dalton." She smiled when he relaxed at her words.

Harold played with his suspenders as he said, "I know Warren and Helen wished they could have come to the ranch with us this morning. You know how much Warren enjoys his interludes here."

"Damn busybody," Frederick said, as he entered the kitchen and poured himself and Dalton cups of coffee. His blue eyes sparkled as he talked about Warren. "He'll find any excuse to sneak onto the ranch for an interlude with his wife."

Dalton shifted from foot to foot and shared a concerned look with his wife. "Won't those have to come to an end now that Lottie and I will move into my old cabin?"

Frederick grinned and nodded for them to follow him. He opened the side door leading toward the barn and whistled. A few hoots were heard in the distance, as though answering Frederick's call.

Irene patted Charlotte one more time and stood from the table. Charlotte scooted out after Irene and linked hands with Dalton. "I don't know what they have planned," she whispered.

"Whatever it is, act delighted," he muttered with a wink. "With our luck, they've found Brutus and decided he should be your pet."

She giggled and leaned against his side. He breathed in her subtle scent and knew that whatever was planned wouldn't take away from this moment.

Frederick allowed his grandparents down the steps but remained, blocking Dalton and Charlotte from leaving the kitchen. "Once you get outside, you'll know what the surprise is. And you'll understand why I wanted you away at the homestead for so long. Don't be mad."

"Mad?" Dalton asked, as he stepped in front of Charlotte. "Oh, what did you do?" he whispered, as he gazed out at the area past the driveway. Rather than two cabins, a newly constructed one sat on the opposite side of Slims and Davina's, away from the one he had shared with Mary. It looked larger, and it had a sizeable front porch.

Sorcha raced toward them, her braid flowing behind her.

"Dalton! Charlotte! Is it no' the bonniest cabin?" She stumbled to a halt, as she saw their dumbfounded expressions. "Do ye no' like it? How can ye no' like it?" She fisted her hands on her hips, as she stared at them in consternation.

Frederick wrapped an arm around her waist, whispering in her ear as he eased her away.

Dalton turned to face his wife, leading her down the steps, his eyes glistening. "It seems our family made us a cabin."

"How?" Charlotte gasped, her eyes huge. "We never meant to be a bother. We could sleep in a room in the bunkhouse."

Sorcha wrapped her in a hug, silencing her protestations.

Frederick slapped Dalton on his back. "I realized you couldn't return to the home you'd shared with Mary. It wouldn't be right for either of you. Besides, Warren needs that for his retreats from town."

Harold swayed on his feet. "Come on! Quit lollygaggin', and come see your new home!" He held out his arm for Irene, and they followed Dalton and Charlotte as they walked arm and arm toward the cabin.

"I can't believe they did this for us," Dalton said over and over again, his gaze taking in the finely constructed cabin. His smile broadened as Ewan emerged from inside with Ben. "Where'd you hide last night?" Dalton called out.

"In the other cabin. Figured we'd be safe there," Ben said, as he shook Dalton's hand.

Dalton clapped Ewan on his back, as he led Charlotte up the porch steps. "The step doesn't dip with my weight."

Ewan laughed. "Aye, that's because we built it."

Poking his head inside, Dalton noted a two-room cabin. Facing his friends, who were also his family, he shook his head in amazement. "I don't know what to say."

Charlotte squeezed his hand, in an instant understanding everything Dalton, Bears, and the family had been trying to teach her. Love and friendship and acts of goodwill from those who truly cared for you were never offered to place you in that person's debt. Charlotte never wanted to honor such precious gifts again with her imaginary tally in her mind. "Thank you. Thank you so much." She let out a deep breath. "I was dreading battling a ghost."

"Enjoy your home. We'll have a proper celebration tonight," Frederick said. "Dalton, take another few days off to enjoy time with your bride. Soon enough you'll have plenty of work." He eased the small group away from the cabin, as Dalton stood on the porch with Charlotte.

"Well, do you want to go in?" he asked.

She shook her head. "No."

"No?" he asked, dumbfounded. "Lottie, this will be our home. They've done this for us. How can you—"

She covered his lips with her fingers, her eyes filled with regret. "I denied us so much on our wedding day. Our first dance. Cutting the cake." Her eyes filled, and she blinked to banish the tears. "But I don't want to lose out on this tradition." She bit her lip. "Will you carry me over the threshold?"

He gave a small *whoop*, sweeping her into his arms. "With pleasure, my love." He kissed her and then eased inside with her in his arms, thankful for a little more free time with her, before he had to return to work.

CHAPTER 16

Dalton lifted his head from the comfortable pillows, frowning at the sound of wagon after wagon rolling down the drive. He eased out from under Charlotte, resting her head on the pillow and kissing her cheek. "I'll be back in a moment," he murmured, as she gave a whimper of protest.

Peering out the front window, he saw the large MacKinnon family and their associates jumping down from the wagons. They smiled and embraced each other, giving Dalton the impression that everything was well. However, never had they all come to the ranch at one time. "Give me a moment, love. I'll be back."

He slipped on his boots and was out the door a moment later, patting down his hair. "Mr. Harold!" he called out. Clutching Harold's hand, he gaped at the sight of Tobias Sutton standing beside him. "Sir, I'm certain you're not welcome here."

"Now don't get on your high horse. It's up to Frederick to decide, and the boy's not noticed yet," Harold said. "Besides, Tobias is a member of the family, and this is a family party."

"A family party?" Dalton asked, momentarily distracted

from the presence of the man who had wreaked such havoc on Frederick's family. "I don't understand."

"Well, when word reached us yesterday about that man finally turnin' up, and then needin' poor Helen's aid last night, we decided it was high time for a party. You and your bride were a bit skittish at your weddin'. Thought it was time for a do-over."

Rubbing his head with exasperation, Dalton muttered, "You can't do-over a wedding, Mr. Harold. We've been married for some time now."

"That might be so, and I hope you've found happiness with her." He paused, staring deeply into Dalton's bright blue eyes. He smiled at whatever he saw in them. "And so it appears you have. However, you never did dance with her. Nor did you eat your cake." He motioned to Annabelle, unloading goodies from the back of the wagon. "Anna's made you another cake, and, if you have the sense I always thought you had, you won't protest."

With a quick shake of his head, Dalton stared at everyone in dumbfounded awe. "They're here for Lottie and me?"

"Yes, lad," Harold said. "Go get your bride. Everyone wants to reassure themselves that she's well. There was quite an uproar last night at the thought she'd been harmed."

Dalton cleared his throat, his eyes tear glazed. "Thank you, sir." He thumped Harold on his back, before striding to his new home, Tobias's presence forgotten. His breath caught. *His new home.* One that he'd share with Lottie. And not have to battle memories of another life. Another time.

He took a steadying breath and opened the door, smiling to find his bride still abed. "Love," he said in a tender voice. "You'll want to get dressed. Our time to lay about has come to an end."

She gazed up at him adoringly. "Why?" she whispered in an enticing way, that always made him want to jump back into bed with her. Then she sat upright, her gaze filled with fear as she panted in panic. "The wagons. It's trouble. He's escaped. He's after me."

Reaching her in a few short strides, Dalton caressed her shoulders. "No, love. Nothing like that." Soothing caresses to her head and hair had her leaning against him. "Never that." He shuddered as he kissed her brow. "The MacKinnons and all the family have come calling. Want to ensure you are well and then have a party to celebrate us."

"Celebrate us?" she asked, pushing back to stare at him in bewilderment. "Why?"

"They want us to dance and eat cake." He frowned as her eyes filled with tears. "I thought it would bring you joy."

She threw herself into his arms, wrapping hers around him with such a ferocious tenderness that he almost lost his breath. "It does." She sniffled, as she refused to let him go. "I'm trying not to be overwhelmed by their generosity."

Kissing her head and running hands over her back, he waited the long moments she needed before she relaxed in his arms. "I want to dance with you. Eat cake with you. Watch you bloom under their love and care."

She looked up at him, shaking her head. "I bloom because of your care, husband."

Sighing, he kissed her, forgetting the large group waiting them. For now, he had everything he wanted in his arms.

Charlotte approached the large group setting up trestle tables with a cautious gait. The women chattered and laughed, their jovial attitude infectious. Smiling, Charlotte asked, "What can I do to help?"

"Charlotte!" Jessamine yelled, pulling her in close for a hug, before releasing her to pass her off to her kinswomen.

Soon Annabelle, Fidelia, Leticia, and Jane had embraced her too—Sorcha and Davina watching with smiles. "Oh, you don't know how relieved I am to see you well!"

"I wanted to bash that man with my rolling pin for daring to harm you," Annabelle said, as she tugged her close. "Cailean wouldn't let me out of his sight."

Helen laughed. "For that, I am grateful. I spent too much time sewing him up. I couldn't have handled having to sew him up again. I have a headache from all his bellyaching as is." She smiled at Charlotte to indicate she was teasing. "I'm glad you're well," she whispered in Charlotte's ear.

After greeting Fidelia, Jane, and Leticia, Charlotte looked at the platters of food and cake. "I never thought we'd need this much food for just us."

"Oh, the men are worse than a horde of locusts," Fidelia said, as she glanced fondly at the men, who stood at the paddock railing, staring at horses, her gaze on Bears and Frederick. She looked at Davina. "Go join them. I know they'd answer your questions, and you can listen in."

Davina attempted to hide her eagerness but betrayed it when she trotted over to them. At their joyful welcome, Fidelia smiled. "Bears is delighted she is interested in horses. He hopes Bright Fawn will be one day too."

Charlotte glanced at the group of contented laughing women, who chatted around her. "It seems we've all been fortunate in the men we've chosen." When she bit her lip, the conversation ceased, and all eyes focused on her. "Oh my, I'm not used to being the center of attention."

"What's the matter?" Jessamine demanded. "What's he done to worry you?"

Rolling her eyes, Charlotte couldn't help smiling dreamily. "Nothing. He's done nothing." She let out a pent-up breath. "I'm worried about Orville. What will happen when he's released? Won't he come back to hurt me?"

Helen shrugged. "He's in custody, and he'll never have full use of his right arm again. He'll be lucky to use a teaspoon."

Jessamine smiled wickedly. "By the time my story runs in the Butte papers, which I sent off to them today, he'll have so much notoriety that he'll tuck tail and run back to Philadelphia. He's got much greater worries, Charlotte."

Shaking her head, Charlotte said, "I don't understand."

Although she attempted to not appear too pleased with herself, Jessamine couldn't hide her satisfaction. "You're fortunate that you're related to the town reporter. And I'm sick and tired of boring tall tales!" She made a groan at the thought of hearing another one. "Thus, when that woman arrived, and then he came to town, I knew something was going on. I never believed the twaddle about your father."

Jessamine paused, looking momentarily chagrined at her frank talk. However, when Charlotte was not offended, Jessamine barreled on. "I dug around and found out through sources that Orville is heavily leveraged. He wanted to compete with the true Copper Kings in Butte, and he borrowed heavily in an attempt to rival them. He's mortgaged past his ears, and now that he won't be a senator and won't write bonuses to himself as a member of Congress, he has no way to pay back his lenders. From what I've learned, they are rather impatient men."

Charlotte stood in dazed wonder. "You mean, I'm finally free of him?" At Jessamine's nod, Charlotte gave a small *whoop* and threw herself in Jessamine's arms. "Thank you!"

Laughing, Jessamine said, "I did nothing. I just wrote the article."

"No, you did so much. You took your time and your tenacity to learn the truth. And that truth has helped me." Charlotte beamed first at Jessamine and then all the women. "Thank you for your friendship."

At that, they shrugged, as though their offer of friendship

and loyalty were not the precious gift it was, and continued to set out food. As Charlotte unwrapped a plate of deviled eggs, Helen turned away, holding her mouth. "Helen? Are you all right?"

"Give me a moment," Helen gasped, striding away. She took deep breaths with her eyes closed, before sitting down in the tall grass.

"Helen!" Sorcha exclaimed, rushing to her. "What's the matter with ye? I'll go for Warren."

Grabbing Sorcha's hand, Helen stilled the woman's frantic movement. "There's no need. He knows all about it. He made me like this."

At her words, the women all smiled. "You mean, ye're finally with bairn?" Sorcha said, as she gave a *whoop* of joy. "Oh, at last! I thought ye'd never have a child."

Helen looked up at them with an abashed smile. "I'm a midwife. I shouldn't be embarrassed. But I am." She shrieked with laughter as Sorcha toppled down beside her to hug her. Soon she'd been hauled to her feet for a massive group hug. "I never thought to have a baby. Not after so many years married with never a missed cycle. And then … this." She held a hand over her belly in wonder.

"You'll be a wonderful mother, Helen," Jessamine said, her eyes glowing. "Oh, this is a true celebration for us all."

"Aye," Sorcha said. "I hope the first of many to come at the ranch."

Later that evening, Frederick stood to the side of the party, watching as Dalton and Charlotte danced together. He knew Annabelle had baked the happy couple a chocolate cake and that they would carve into it soon. Although they'd had their formal wedding over a month ago, this gathering with the family seemed to be their true celebration. They were deeply in love, and he was thankful the weeks away at the small homestead had given them the time they needed to repair whatever damage Adella had done.

"You seem mighty satisfied with yourself," his uncle said, as he sauntered toward him.

Frederick stiffened. "Remind me again why you were allowed to return to the ranch." He spoke in a low voice, laced with anger.

"Jane is here. She invited me." Tobias nodded toward his daughter, laughing and dancing with her husband on the makeshift dance floor. "Seemed churlish to turn down her invitation."

"No," Frederick snapped, as he faced his uncle. "You've searched for any reason to defy my command that you were, and always will be, barred from this ranch." Although Jane was also Frederick's cousin, and there was little Frederick would deny her, he wished he were cruel enough to force Tobias away in the middle of a party.

Tobias sighed, his bravado cracking, as he beheld his beloved nephew. "Please, Frederick. I've known what it is to be a part of family again with Jane. With the MacKinnons. Don't you understand how I long for it with you? With your brothers?"

Shaking his head with astounded incredulity, Frederick took a step away from his uncle. "How dare you?" he whispered. "You had everything, Uncle. Everything." He swallowed and blinked his eyes, as though on the verge of losing control of his deepest emotions. "And you threw it all away. You threw us away."

"It wasn't like that, Frederick. I promise you." Tobias held out his hands, pleading with his nephew to understand.

"Tell me what it was like," said another, his low voice

laced with a deep anger. "Tell me before I knock you on your behind for darin' to be here."

"Peter!" Frederick gasped, launching himself at his brother. "What are you doing here?" He looked around in confusion. "Where's Cole? The herd? What's going on?" He stared at his eldest brother, who stood tall and twitching with the urge to pummel their uncle. Frederick and Peter were of similar height, although Peter's hair was chestnut colored, rather than black. They shared the same blue eyes.

Peter looked momentarily chagrined. "It's a long story, Fred." He glanced around at the ongoing festivities. "I never thought I'd arrive in the middle of a celebration. Is that Dalton dancin' with a woman?"

Grinning, Frederick said, "His wife."

At the mention of a wife, Peter paled. "Don't mention wives. Or preachers." He shook his head. "I've had a devil of a time escapin' both."

"What?" Frederick gasped. "You've always excelled at flirtin' with the ladies but never letting it lead to anything serious. What happened?"

Peter shook his head again, focusing on their uncle. "That's a story for another day too. Right now I'd like to know why he's here. And if he's finally told you the truth about what happened all those years ago with Mother." He nodded with bitter delight when he saw their uncle pale. "That's right, Tobias. I learned the truth. Imagine my surprise."

"No," Tobias breathed. "Not here. Don't ruin the celebration. It's not fair to … to Dalton." He stumbled over the name, as though he had almost forgotten who had just married.

When Peter motioned for Frederick to remain quiet, he bit back a litany of questions. As the youngest brother, Frederick found some habits were hard to break. "Fine, Uncle. But, come tomorrow, there will be a reckoning."

After Tobias scurried away, Frederick watched him with unveiled loathing. "I'll have one of the hands ensure he doesn't attempt to sneak away in the middle of the night."

Peter nodded. "It's good to be back, Fred. I fear we'll be here forever now. The time of the open range is behind us."

Frederick nodded. "We'll figure somethin' out Come. Let's celebrate with Dalton. Eat cake. And you can see how my bairns have grown. They've missed their uncle Peter." Frederick clapped a hand on his brother's shoulder, attempting to ignore the deep sense of foreboding filling him for what would be revealed.

Charlotte stood in Dalton's arms, swaying to the sound of a fiddle. She rested her head on his shoulder, ignoring the laughter, the quiet conversation, and the general sense of joy that permeated the air. "Are you happy?" she whispered into his ear.

"Happy?" he asked, his soft lips trailing over her neck and provoking a shiver. "No, love. I'm ecstatic. Euphoric." He grinned at her, his hold on her tightening. "I think I need to borrow Miss Jessamine's thesaurus to find all the words to describe how I feel with you here in my arms tonight."

She giggled, staring into his gaze, as though everything had faded away, and only the two of them danced near the flickering light from the bonfire.

"I love that sound," he murmured, raising one hand to trace over her lips. "It means, you're happy too."

"No," she teased, arching up to kiss him. "Enraptured. Blissful." She giggled again when he chuckled.

"I guess I don't need the reporter's book. I just need you."

He paused as his words settled around them. "I just need you, Lottie."

She sobered, gazing deeply into his earnest gaze. "I know," she breathed. "I need you too, my love. Forever and always."

"For no other reason than because you are precious to me," he murmured, burying his head in her hair. He twined his arms around her.

"As you are to me. I love you, Dalton. I've loved you for so long. I'll love you forever."

His arms tightened on her back, and he swayed both of them to the music. "Ah, Lottie, love. As long as we are together, we can face anything. Anything, my beloved."

A scorned woman seeking retribution. A shamed man, haunted by his past with no hope for the future. When their paths collide, will they overcome their animosity to find love?

P eter Tompkins has always had a greater affinity for cattle than women. Although a notorious flirt, he has little faith in the steadfastness of a woman's love. After his mother's betrayal, and his family's heartache, he learned that to place his trust in a woman is to endanger his heart. Thus, upon his return home to his family's ranch, he is dumbfounded to learn his attempt to evade Philomena Fitch has failed.

P hilomena Fitch is dismayed her brother accepted a position in Bear Grass Springs. Now, she will have to confront the man who betrayed her. Who made a fool of her. Who broke her heart. When she uncovers the truth behind his actions, she must decide if she can forgive him and learn to trust in him again.

When the past is resurrected to wreak havoc on the present, Peter and Philomena must decide if they prefer to cling to disappointment or dare to dream of a resplendent future. **Will they have faith in the love growing between them or will they allow the betrayals of the past to keep them apart?**

Order Now! Available March 2021!

DON'T MISS A RAMONA FLIGHTNER UPDATE!

Thank you for reading *Pioneer Longing*! I hope you enjoyed it as much as I enjoyed writing it.

I love hearing from you, so please feel free to write me and let me know what you think!

You can reach me at: ramona@ramonaflightner.com

Join My Newsletter For Updates, and Sneak Peeks about the series you love!

Want new release alerts, access to bonus materials and exclusive giveaways, and all my announcements first? Subscribe to my weekly newsletter!

Want to be notified about freebies and sales? Try Bookbub!

Want to stay up to date on new releases, my life in beautiful Montana, and research trip adventures? Follow my hashtag

#ramonasmontanalife to follow along with my adventures as I post gorgeous pictures and videos of my life in Montana. Find Me On Facebook! Or Find Me On Instagram!

ALSO BY RAMONA FLIGHTNER

The O'Rourke Family Montana Saga

Follow the O'Rourke Family as they settle in Fort Benton, Montana Territory in 1865. Coming in 2020!

Sign up here to receive the prequel, *Pioneer Adventure* to the new Saga as a thank you for subscribing to my newsletter!

Pioneer Dream (OFMS, Book 1)- Kevin and Aileen

Pioneer Desire- (OFMS, Book 2)- Ardan and Deirdre

Pioneer Yearning- (OFMS, Book 3) Niamh and Cormac

Pioneer Longing (OFMS, Book 4)- August 2020! Eamon's story!

Pioner Bliss (OFMS, Book 5) Coming January 2021! Declan's story!

Pioneer Devotion (OFMS, Book 6) Maggie's story! Coming in 2021!

Bear Grass Springs Series

Never fear, I am busy at work on the next book in the series! If you want to make sure you never miss a release, a special, a cover reveal, or a short story just for my fans, sign up for my newsletter!

Immerse yourself in 1880's Montana as the MacKinnon siblings and their extended family find love!

Montana Untamed (BGS, Book 1)- Cailean and Annabelle

Montana Grit (BGS, Book 2)- Alistair and Leticia

Montana Maverick (BGS, Book 3) Ewan and Jessamine

Montana Renegade(BGS, Book 4) Warren and Helen

Jubilant Montana Christmas (BGS, Book 5) Leena and Karl

Montana Wrangler (BGS, Book 6) Sorcha and Frederick

Unbridled Montana Passion (BGS, Book 7) Fidelia and Bears

Montana Vagabond (BGS, Book 8) Ben and Jane

Exultant Montana Christmas (BGS, Book 9) Ewan and Jessamine

Lassoing a Montana Heart (BGS, Book 10) Slims and Davina

Healing Montana Love (BGS, Book 11) Dalton and Charlotte

Runaway Montana Groom (BGS, Book 12) Coming in March 2021!

The Banished Saga

Follow the McLeod, Sullivan and Russell families as they find love, their loyalties are tested, and they overcome the challenges of their time. A sweeping saga set between Boston and Montana in early 1900's America. Finally, the Saga is complete!

The Banished Saga: (In Order)

Love's First Flames (Prequel)

Banished Love

Reclaimed Love

Undaunted Love (Part One)

Undaunted Love (Part Two)

Tenacious Love

Unrelenting Love

Escape To Love

Resilient Love

Abiding Love

Triumphant Love

ABOUT THE AUTHOR

Ramona is a historical romance author who loves to immerse herself in research as much as she loves writing. A native of Montana, every day she marvels that she gets to live in such a beautiful place. When she's not writing, her favorite pastimes are fly fishing the cool clear streams of a Montana river, hiking in the mountains, and spending time with family and friends.

Ramona's heroines are strong, resilient women, the type of women you'd love to have as your best friend. Her heroes are loyal and honorable, men you'd love to meet or bring home to introduce to your family for Sunday dinner. She hcpes her stories bring the past alive and allow you to forget the outside world for a while.

BB bookbub.com/authors/ramona-flightner
f facebook.com/authorramonaflightner
⟨O⟩ instagram.com/rflightner
℗ pinterest.com/Ramonaauthor

www.ingramcontent.com/pod-product-compliance
Lightning Source LLC
Chambersburg PA
CBHW022137240626
47153CB00007B/2399